PRAISE F(

"..... an excellent read.... such an outstanding book..... a job well done..... The book brought tears to my eyes...."

—**Sonny Blacks:** Artistic Director, Commonwealth Arts & Cultural Foundation—London, U K.

"I thoroughly enjoyed Curry Cascadoo. .....I liked the combination of standard and non-standard (Trini) English.....each episode read like a short story in its own right.... nostalgia for the homeland struck a very responsive chord, and the easy flow of the text should appeal to all..... The eventual reconciliation is well done.... inspiring work."

—**Keith Q Warner:** Author of several books and Professor Emeritus of French and Caribbean Studies at George Mason University, Fairfax, Virginia

"Every page of this book vibrates with a deep love and longing for the islands, Trinidad to be specific....through his writing, we are taken on a heart-rending ride of pathos and joy....With marvelous restraint, through poetic reflections and recollections of youth, the author helps us to gradually realize the voice's impending tragic end."

—**Tony Hall:** Playwright, Producer, Director, and Co-Founder of Lordstreet Theatre Company

"This story is written in an easy almost seductive style.... excellent use of language... extended sentences utilized with maximum effect... Poetry and prose offer a most intriguing format which demonstrates the writer's creative versatility...A most enjoyable read!"

—**Indra Ribeiro:** Image Consultant, Former External Advice Columnist with the Trinidad Express Newspapers, PRO of the United Nations Association of Trinidad & Tobago

"I love the multi-layered nature of the story and the way the apparently disparate pieces come together as the story progresses..... I liked the prose pieces, and the musical and lyrical flow of the pieces written in Trini dialect..."

—**Nazru Deen:** Retired Superintendent of Education, Ottawa District School Board, Canada.

"I thoroughly enjoyed the book .....brought back memories of long ago....An important lesson for all of us."

Dianne Phillips: Manager, WACK 90.1 FM-Radio, San Fernando, Trinidad.

"The Trini reminiscences are explosive and joyful...Words and images tumbling over one another in a truly musical and celebratory mix, rich with the author's love of his homeland.....The New York passages are claustrophobic and tight, morbidly final and heartbreaking...."

—**James Whitmore:** Actor/ Director, Hollywood, California

"This little book packs a powerful punch! The style is unique. The prose is simple and direct. The poetry is beautiful ...provides compelling storytelling throughout. I was particularly struck by the end which, although tragic, still managed to convey a sense of hope and reconciliation. ....certainly a book for everyone!!"

—**Ingrid Barclay John-Baptiste**, President Trinidad & Tobago Ottawa Association, Host of Caribbean Calender on Rogers Television

"..... interesting reading....the use of dialect gives the book a nice flavor.... the poetry was beautiful! Really well written...I have enjoyed reading this book."

—**Waheeda Deen:** National Library & Information System Authority of Trinidad & Tobago. (NALIS).

"I quite like the format and the mixture of poetry and prose .... The themes of emptiness, loneliness, displacement, disappointment come through very well.... The interplay between time and place was quite skillful..... A good read that takes the reader on an introspective journey about his/her own life, dreams, desires, passions and begs one to consider the question: what have I done with my life."

—**Joanne Haynes:** CEO of Pepperpot Productions, Educator and Author of "Walking" and the award winning "Sapotee Soil"

"....Very enjoyable reading.... brings back a lot of memories about growing up in the Caribbean..."

—**Milton Zaiffdeen:** Operations Lead, Shell Oil Company, Edmonton, Alberta, Canada.

"An intriguing read, the way the author blends the local dialect in ...creates 'a nice callaloo' ... an enjoyable trip down memory lane.... One can just close ones eyes and travel back in time."

—**Dr. Safeeya Mohammed- Bhagan:** Paedritic Medical Doctor

"...a virtual novel on a Trinidad past.....the stories would make very good storytelling performances .....vivid, tactile and delicious."

—**Rhoma Spencer:** Artistic Director Theatre Archipelago – Toronto, Canada

" I love Curry Cascadoo. The experiences are uniquely similar to mine and written as if just for me..... great beginning, compelling middle and a surprising yet dynamic end."

—**Michael Jobe:** Consultant and Advisor at Georgetown and Emory Universities in the US and to Community Groups and Government Ministries in Trinidad & Tobago.

"Very nice and easy read ....provoked memories for those of us who have migrated from the Caribbean to metropolitan cities .....I rather enjoyed this pleasant walk down memory lane."

—**Hazra Ali:** CEO of New Hope & Beyond Inc. and Community Activist; Brooklyn, New York.

"... takes the reader on a beautiful journey..... Both his story writing and his poems take on a melodic tone that makes for delightful reading..... his love for his homeland is conveyed throughout."

—**Diana Zaiffdeen:** T&T Compatriot and Single Parent who, against tremendous odds, successfully raised two highly professional sons. Edmonton, Alberta, Canada

"I felt like it was my story.......being alone and missing families back home during seasons of celebration are experiences that many of us should share.......it will certainly touch the lives of many ......Your 'cascadoo' is really sweet!... One will surely come back for more!"

—**Nana Mensah Abrampa 1** (Lynton Raphael): Nkosuohene of Yamfo in Brong Ahafo Region of Ghana. Member of the African Mobilisation Committee. Founding member of Sonatas Steel Orchestra of NY. Taught at Universities in NYC and Ghana.

Curry Cascadoo

a story

Kamalo Deen

PEMPALEH INTERNATIONAL PRODUCTIONS

Copyright © 2011 Kamalo Deen

All rights reserved. No part of this publication may be reproduced, stored in a retrieval system, or transmitted in any form or by any means, electronic, mechanical, photocopying, recording or otherwise without the prior permission of the author.

ISBN 978-0-9859654-0-2

Published by:
Pempaleh International Productions
86 Robin Road, Staten Island, New York 10305
Tel:718-442-8977

Email: kiss_deen@verizon.net
www.pempaleh.com

Cover design by Ishmael Deen

Printed by: Gorham Printing 3718 Mahoney Drive, Centralia, WA98531. Tel:1-800-837-0970

For Sherma

FOREWORD

Throughout history, people have travelled away from their homes in pursuit of distant hopes and dreams.

This story is inspired by the ones, who having left, never lost hope that someday they would return.

This is a work of fiction whose sole purpose is to entertain by offering an insight into some of the activities, recollections and reflections of one such fictional character.

In my capacity as storyteller I have taken several liberties with this presentation to ensure the consistent flow of the narrative.

Persons, places and events actively depicted here are not meant to represent or resemble any real persons, places or events, past or present.

Kamalo Deen

Curry Cascadoo - A Story

PROLOGUE

She was sixty seven years old when she left our village to live with her daughter and grand children in St Lucia.

Her son was a doctor in England and she had visited him and his family on two occasions but she said she just couldn't see herself living over there.

She didn't care to live in St Lucia either but her daughter convinced her that since it was also an island in the Caribbean she shouldn't find it to be much different to home.

I had known her for eight years, ever since our family had moved to her village, into the house next door to where she and her husband lived.

I suppose she had taken a liking to me because I was young and inquisitive and would make time to sit and talk with her every day. I told her that I was determined to become a writer and she seemed pleased to hear that. She liked to talk about her childhood in the village, growing up with her parents and her brother who she said had once been a writer himself, in New York.

Her husband had died of the flu the year after we'd moved in and despite constant demands and pleadings by her daughter and grandchildren, it took almost seven years for her to finally and reluctantly agree to sell the house and join them.

From the moment she made her decision she seemed to age considerably. Her movements became slower and she spoke softly with a tone that alternated between resignation and pain. She gave the impression of someone in deep conflict, torn between two unyielding loves, wanting on the one hand to be with her family but on the other, unwilling to sever ties with her past.

During her last two weeks in the house I'd helped her pack her belongings. Some she'd arranged to be sent to St Lucia but most she gave away to friends and neighbors in the village.

The day before she left there was a constant flow of people coming to say goodbye and to wish her a safe trip. There was much hugging and kissing and tears and at times even some laughter.

When things finally quieted down that evening and we were alone sharing what would be our last cup of coffee at her home, she brought out a medium-sized cardboard box from her bedroom and handed it to me.

"What is it?" I asked her.

"It's my brother's," she said simply. "It means a lot to me. I want you to try to do something good with it."

As soon as I got home that night I opened the box. It contained eighteen notebooks and several neatly wrapped stacks of paper consisting mainly of letters and cards sent and received. Since then I've read and re-read the contents of that box several times. In it is a fascinating collection of poems, plays, short stories, ideas, letters, recollections and an unfinished novel.

What follows here are his words. All I did was select particular items from the material in the box, do some editing and then arrange them in a continuous format to convey the story.

HIS STORY

...in his own words...

ONE

When the first gray light of morning fills the east
And tiny white clouds embrace the distant mountaintops
And the hurrying insects and the singing birds
Give life to a sleeping world;
When the soft green leaves
And the multi-colored flowers
And the slender blades of grass
Reflect from their gathered dewdrops
The first rays of the rising sun;
When the village awakens and fishermen hurry
To the wailing call of the conch-shell;
Then I, prisoner of freedom that I am,
With anxious steps, climb the highest slope.
And there, like a monarch over all the land,
Gazing at the wild ocean to the north and east;
There, with the gurgling sounds of mountain streams
Whispering quiet love-chants
To the frolicking creatures
And the flitting clouds
And the forest trees,
I contemplate on the strange destiny that must lie before me;
And with each passing moment my heart convinces me more,

*That I must break these chains of freedom
Which have bound me so long,
And wander through the great cities
Far across the northern sea;
And there, like a timid lamb in the jungle,
I must become a part of the race.*

TWO

December 19th 1979

Dear Sis,

The streets of New York are alive with pre-Christmas paraphernalia. The spirit, with its holly and mistletoe, its ringing bells and singing minstrels, its street corner sidewalk santas and over-decorated department store windows, is extremely vast and elaborate. No pains are spared to create this atmosphere of fantasy; this buzzing, bubbling specter of human imagination.

This is a grand time here; a time of snowflakes drifting and spirits lifting; of vendors hustling and shoppers bustling; of crammed-up subways and jammed-up traffic-ways; of sirens screaming and sidewalks teeming and lovers dreaming and children beaming.

It's a time of laughing loudly and stepping proudly; of joyous chatter and store-sales clatter; of Yule-logs toasting and chestnuts roasting; of charming faces and warm embraces and skidoo races and Saks showcases.

It's a playing time and a sleighing time; a skating time and a mating time; a living time and a giving time; a hearty time and a party time. It's a time of celebrating and congregating; inebriating and integrating; a time when the spirit yearns to roam; a time when I long again for home.

I long for the simple, long-time Christmas among friends and relatives.

I long for the taste of homemade ginger beer and the smell of black cakes and sponge cakes and fruit cakes and egg cakes, baking outside in firewood ovens.

I long for the pastelle and paymee; the curry duck and dhal-puree; the tum-tum and calaloo; the pelau, macaroni pie and corn coocoo; the roast pork, bulljoll and boiled ham; the river fish and wild-meat stew with eddoes, dasheen, green fig and yam.

I long for mauby, punch-a-creme, seamoss and eggnog; for coconut, barbadine or soursop ice-cream, and a petit-quart of Puncheon or Old Oak grog; for the box of apples and grapes hidden underneath the bed; the sugar cakes and pawpaw candies, coconut drops and sweet bread; for the nuts, the prunes, the dates, the milk fudge and the tambran ball; the Christmas cards hanging in a curved line along the living room wall.

I long for the carolers' candlelight harmonies; the paranderos' cuatro melodies; the pan, the tassa, the dhantal and the dholak; the tide bucket, the bottle-and-spoon, the Bermudez biscuit drum and the shak-shak.

I long for the bamboo guns and carbile blasting through open flames; the women's chatter, the old men's stories, the children's joyous and noisy games...I long for home.

Throughout his life a man may live in various places, yet there's only one to which he always looks, as home. I wish I was there now among the people who'd watched over me as I grew. But this can't be, so I must try to not occupy my mind with such thoughts, for they serve only to enhance my loneliness, exacerbate my health problems and make me more miserable than I already am.

Except for my job at the plant, I spend most of my time now, absorbed in my writing. There's so much to say and so little time left to say it.

Time, how quickly it's slipped by. So many years feigning satisfaction; so many years pursuing elusive themes; so many years of planning with little action; so many years squandered on idle dreams.

Though death constantly surrounds us, we live with the delusion that life will go on forever, so whenever possible we postpone duties, thus placing too heavy a burden on the future.

I can delay no longer. My pen is insistent. My mind is on fire. There's a constant turmoil in my breast; a raging inferno which seems to be dragging me along at will. Where it's all leading to, I don't know. So for the time being, I close my eyes to the rocks and rapids in my path as I rush along with the current. Only time will tell if it will all fizzle away in the heat of some distant desert, or whether at the next turn, the vast and raging ocean awaits, with wide-open arms, my arrival.

THREE

There is a song locked in my soul
That struggles to be free.
There is a fire in my eyes
That no one seems to see.
There is a dream inside my heart
That grows with each day's dawning.
There is a voice from deep within
That's calling ever calling.

FOUR

December 22nd

I often wonder about how quickly my once vibrant life had tumbled then catapulted into its present state.

I used to be relevant. I used to be liked and respected. I was always in the thick of things. People used to seek my advice, both back home and here in this country. My door was always open to all, and many availed themselves of my hospitality. Then it had all evaporated…. Pffft…; vanished into thin air!

I'm not sure exactly when the metamorphosis began; when I started this retreat into myself. The one thing I'm certain of, however, is that deep down in my gut I'd always felt that it was going to happen.

Even during my life at home when I was surrounded by the family and the community, and then later on during my time here with Joyce, while I was spoiled and pampered and stifled within the boundaries of security, I'd always felt the proximity of an approaching gloom. Now that area of darkness deep down inside, which had always beckoned, is overpowering me and I must steel myself for the outcome.

I just got off work and am on the south bound number one train heading home to my apartment. I'm sitting in a corner seat sucking on a Vicks cherry-flavored cough drop in an effort to stifle the heaving in my throat. It's a constant battle I have to wage against the need to emit a racking, rattling cough while in the proximity of strangers. Whenever I fail and it escapes I can sense the curious and sometimes disapproving stares from others in my vicinity so now, just in case I don't succeed in suppressing it, I keep my eyes closed and pretend to be asleep.

    The train is crowded at this time of day. At each stop I can see, through slight cracks in my closed eyelids, crowds of people hustling out through the open doors while crowds more squeeze in. Everyone, coming or going, seems anxious to get somewhere. Some are carrying shopping bags displaying department store logos indicating that they were out doing their Christmas shopping. Most are hurrying home from work, perhaps to retire for the day or maybe to grab a bite to eat before hustling out again to begin their assault on the enticing seasonal displays advertised everywhere.

    Although it's the beginning of the week and our annual Christmas party, in the company's cafeteria, won't be held until Thursday, they paid us early to allow us enough time to do our Christmas shopping. The company is pretty good that way. We also got our Christmas bonus and since we're an umbrella manufacturing plant each employee received a large family-size beach umbrella. Every year we get one of these so I have five of them now in various colors in a closet in my apartment.

FIVE

The first time I ever went to Piarco Airport was to see mih cousin Mangohead off. He was going to England during the time when plenty Trinis was trying to beat the August Independence deadline.

Well I tell you, I never see nothing so! People in the airport like peas! All kinds of friends and family was there. The airport was ram-cram and the way some of them feteing and carrying on, you go swear they was glad to get rid of him.

Whiskey and roti was flowing outside in the parking lot like if was a real big shot wedding. And talk about noise! Coolie-people and nigger-people is real never-see-come-see yes! You should see how they getting on in the place! Some of them shouting to one another across the whole airport, and they joking and laughing hard hard, like when they liming by Achang rumshop on the junction.

Mangohead mother was crying non-stop like if was his funeral, and his father was walking around and sweating in his suit and tie and boasting to anyone who go listen, about how his son was going to England to study to be a doctor.

I hear his mother-in-law telling him, "Doh go dere and pick-up no English 'ooman, yuh know. Neighbor Harry say how all dem 'ooman in England does throw dey-self at West Indian man. Doh forget yuh leaving Sheila and the baby over here!"

And they taking pictures like if it was going out of style self! I sure, in his whole life, he never take out so much pictures like that day; everybody rushing to pose for picture with him. And kiss and handshake and hug-up flying like rain! He nearly miss the flight because of all the kissing and hug-up and handshake.

When they start announcing that all passengers must board the flight, everybody start to push and crowd around him, wishing him well and offering last minute advice about the food he should eat and the friends he should keep and clothes he should wear for the weather over there and almost anything else they could think about, although I bet none of them never even gone to Tobago before.

The last person he talk to before he leave, was his wife Sheila. She and all was crying and is only when he hold the baby that I see the tears fulling up his eyes. When he hand Sheila the baby and turn around and start to board the plane, everything turn old mas! Sheila scream out and faint away one time. His mother and mother-in-law start bawling hard hard, like if they was going competition. His father was quarrelling and telling them to behave themselves but he and all had long-long tears running down his face.

All the feteing stop one time and the whole place get quiet. Everybody eyes full up too, and though I was just a little boy at the time, I feel a burning inside mih belly and mih heart start pounding hard-hard-hard in mih chest, because I realize at that moment, for the very first time in mih young life, that behind all the wild feteing and all the bacchanal behavior and the never-see come-see attitude, we people is a good people, a close people, with plenty feelings for we friends and family.

SIX

December 24th

It snowed last night, so I'll be spending another white Christmas. It's no big thing though, because since I'm alone and have no one to see and no special place to go, the day will be spent like any other.

The frequent bouts of coughing have become a part of my life, but I'm still not accustomed to these episodes of depression I face at holiday times. When I'm engulfed in my work I'm fine, but at times like this, it's difficult for me to concentrate.

I haven't written much during the past few days but I did manage to complete a one-act play I'd been working on for some time. It is set in 1932 in Port of Spain and focuses on a chance meeting between Eric Williams and Rudranath Capildeo, while they were both students at Queens Royal College. Williams is in his final year and Capildeo is in his first.

In my story, they meet after school, at a bus stop by the Savannah and strike up a conversation. In it we get a view of two very different approaches to similar goals and a fictional insight into what might've motivated the minds of a future historian and a future mathematician.

It also explores the factors affecting students from the country districts and students from the town in those days, and how their differing racial, religious, community and family values might impact on the colony in the future. It's an interesting piece and took quite a bit of effort. Soon, I hope to approach my novel again.

My novel... For the past five years, ever since I began to seriously pursue my writing again, I've had an on and off relationship with this project.

Sometimes I'd been gung-ho about it but I'd never been able to commit myself long enough to bring it to completion.

Every time in the past, after I'd worked on it for a while, I'd always ended up getting bored or pushing it aside to pursue other ideas. A major problem for me is that although there's a constant flow of ideas bombarding my brain I lack the discipline to commit fully to any one of them for a long enough period of time. Now however, that my novel is again alive and kicking up a storm in my head, I hope I can stay focused long enough to finally complete it.

I received your card today but was disappointed not to find a letter enclosed. It's been five weeks since I got the last one. I know how busy you must be, preparing your family for the Christmas, and I don't wish to impose too much, but I do appreciate whenever you write.

I hope you're not vexed with me because of my reply to your last letter. You have to understand how desperate I feel sometimes. I'm mostly alone. I don't see any of my old acquaintances. I'm not well. And so far I've produced little of any real substance to show for my efforts here as a writer.

Maybe you were right. Maybe it's foolish of me to be living like this. But this is how things have turned out. The truth is, I'd give anything for the life I used to have with Joyce. I should've married her when I had the opportunity. If we'd had a child, things might've been different. I still feel guilty that I'd cheated her of motherhood. Whenever I'd said so to her, she'd tried to reassure me by joking that I was her baby and that I often acted like it too!... God how I miss her!!

Today was our annual Christmas party at work. They stopped all operations at lunchtime and we gathered in the cafeteria where there was music and food and drinks. I had some cranberry juice and a turkey sandwich but was not in a celebratory mood. Afterwards a couple of my co-workers invited me to spend Christmas day tomorrow with their families but I declined.

My walk home from the subway afterwards was slow and tiring. The snow was deep and the wind was biting. On my way I stopped by the corner bodega and got an apple, some grapes, a packet of dates, a small carrot cake, a pint of pistachio ice cream and a large bottle of Harvey's for my Christmas.

I'm sitting by the window writing this letter. I can hear the shouts of neighborhood children playing in the snow outside. I see them slipping and sliding and tossing snowballs at one another and at the passing buses. Music and laughter drift out of every window. Sounds of merriment fill the air, but how they torment me!

SEVEN

When we was small, we use to take we mas-playing real serious. We use to take it so serious, that for weeks before Carnival, we playing Wild Indian and Jab-Jab behind school during recess time. Of course in them days, we ent getting to play no mas on Carnival days, but in school we more than making-up for that.

All the mas players in we band was boys. No girls was allowed. And so they use to be vex for that! But that was we rules. Strictly no girls allowed!! They had their Bazaar Queen and May Queen competitions and we never used to complain about that. That was their thing and this was we thing. So when you see carnival time come around, all the boys used to be strutting around like peacocks, preening and showing off we fancy costumes to everyone including all the girls who would still gather to see us though they was green with envy. Every year we costumes used to get prettier and prettier because we use to put endless effort into we mas preparations. Schoolwork and homework use to have to take a back seat to costume design and preparation until after Carnival over.

The first thing we use to do was get a plain-color pants and shirt or one of we mother's white dress or even a flour bag bedsheet to use as a basic costume. Then we use to decorate it with all kinds of shiny buttons and ribbons and rhinestones and things. Then we use to pick them little grey jumbie beads from behind the Anglican church, because they have a hole running straight down the middle from top to bottom, so we could pass a needle and thread through them to make chains for around we necks. Then we use to take chicken feathers and paint them in different colors with we watercolor set, and glue them on an old hat to make crowns to wear on we heads. Then we use to go up in the lash-patch by the cemetery on the hill near school, and break lash, and beat it on the road, and dry it, and platt it to make whips.

And when you see we go up in the cricket ground on the hill behind school and put on we costumes and we crowns and bead-chains and start cracking we whips and marching around and chanting "Gran failure katoo mama", it was like real mas self.

Plenty people start coming to see us, so we use to show-off too bad! The whole school start packing-up on the school hill recess time and lunch hour just to see us. We was the talk of the village. And we teachers was real proud too!

Mr Lezama, we Principal even write a report telling the Inspector how with his guidance (although he didn't support us in the beginning), we was promoting the arts and culture of the country, and how all the other schools should take pattern from us. We even make the Guardian one time. They had a picture of the whole band posing in front the school in full costume. And Mr. Lezama was most present in the front and center of that picture. I tell you, we was instant heroes in school; and in the whole village too.

By the time I was in Standard Five we d'done do this for three years straight. Everybody was sure that this woulda become a traditional thing every year before Carnival….But you know how Trinidad is a follow-fashion place already; what monkey see monkey do!

That year the boys from the up-the-hill Government school decide that they want to put out their own band too, and that was trouble self! A whole rivalry thing start-up. And what make matters worse, was that plenty of the fellas in we band had brothers and cousins and neighbors in the next school band and the rivalry reach quite home with them because the fellas from each band was trying to sabotage and outdo the fellas from the next band. Was big, big war they fighting at home over their mother's needle and thread or their father's old garden hat.

Man, they scrambling all over the house, looking for anything they could find to fancy-up their costumes, raiding their mother's sewing machine drawers in search of any stray buttons and sequins and things. But is the fowl and them that was really having a hard time. Some of them fellas ent have no shame at all. They almost plucking their mother's setting fowls and laying fowls while they still sitting down on their eggs. And they chasing the yard-cock the family saving for Easter, just to pull out their tail feathers and wing feathers to add to their crowns; and when their mother asking them why the fowl and them bawling and cackling so hard and making so much ruckshun in the place, they blaming it on manicou and big rat. That Carnival must be set a record for how much bare-bamsee yard-cocks we village ever had.

Anyway, that year, in the beginning, it start off as an innocent, show-off thing, with we costumes and chanting and thing, but after a couple of weeks, it start getting real serious. Own, own brothers and next-door neighbors and best friends stop talking altogether, and start watching one another cut-eye, and start picking on one another for fight. For nothing at all some of them raging up and snapping at one another like mama-dog in heat.

To tell you the truth, I really ent know who challenge who, or who arrange the whole thing. All I know, is that word start to spread among the students, that the two bands was going to clash by Angie Street junction, Carnival Friday evening after school.

By the time we parents and them hear what was going on, and them and all the teachers and students from the two schools, and the rest of the people from the village reach up there, the place was like a real battle zone. All the boys from the two bands was dress-up in we full costumes, jumping around like a bunch of wild people, cracking we whips and pelting lash at one another and chanting hard hard like if we gone crazy.

At first the adults try to part us, but when they realize that things was already out of hand and they was just wasting their time, they take a turn on one another. I tell you, was real confusion in the place. Teachers from one school blaming teachers from the next school. Parents cussing-up parents. Teachers blaming parents. Parents blaming teachers. All of them shouting and pointing up in one another face. The way things was going it look like if the adults was ready to grab we whips from us and start raining blows on one another.

The one or two big people who still try to stop the fighting had to brakes lash, trying to pull us apart. But by the time they finally part us and stop the whole thing, most of us had big, big whales all over we backs and legs and arms. Some of the little fellas was crying and chanting at the same time, but they still trying to crack whip and pelt lash. Finally police had to come and break up everything and send everybody home.

It take a long time before things get back to normal in we village again. That incident put an immediate end to we Carnival celebrations in school, and a serious vexing develop between we school and the up-the-hill Government school.

Because of what happen that day, we stop having we Sports Day and we Christmas treat together with them, and we use to have to cross the road anytime we see any teachers or students from that school on the same side with us. Even the two principals stop talking to one another, and to boot, they was president and secretary of the Village Brotherhood and Sisterhood Friendly Society.

Things get really sour for everybody for a while after that. But the worst part for us was, that from that time on, we was never again allowed to leave the school compounds during recess time, or to ever again go up in the lash patch near the cemetery on the hill behind we school.

EIGHT

December 28th

When I awoke this morning to greet the New Year my first inclination was to write to you. The past two weeks have been one long nightmare. My cough is growing worse. Most times it's just a scratchy, stifled sensation, wheezing and bubbling at the base of my throat, escaping only in short, muffled, rattling spurts. But sometimes, it bursts out with such fury from within my chest that I feel like my lungs would explode.

Things aren't going well at the job either. The company is declining and Dave doesn't take advice from any of his employees. When he took over from his father last April, he introduced all these ideas that he'd probably picked up at business school. Within six months the whole culture of the company had changed. Because of a dip in the economy he brought in a consulting firm, which changed the company's focus from aggressive marketing to stringent budgeting. We've been in a slide ever since. Now he spends most of his time in his office, discussing new strategies with the consultants, poring over all of the company's records, studying each department's operating costs and seeking more ways to save money. Yet he continues to lose market while spending a fortune on these consultants.

He cut raw materials, overtime, delivery costs and personnel while orders were slow, and now that the economy has picked up again and orders are increasing, we're caught short-staffed, and this is affecting the quality and delivery-times of our products. Some of our most solid clients, especially the ones who order large quantities of promotional umbrellas, have become so frustrated they've started taking their work elsewhere.

Lately also, he's been getting on my case because of my coughing. He called me into the office last Friday to tell me that some of the other workers are complaining. He said that I must do something about it. In spite of all of that, he's a good boss and seems to be truly concerned about my health.

Yesterday I received another rejection slip for "An Echo Within". It's the usual……*We regret to inform you that although we found your story interesting, it's not the type of subject matter which, in our opinion, will appeal to our readership…* This is now the eleventh for this story. I'd tried re-writing a few of my stories to fit what I thought might be a more acceptable style, but I wasn't satisfied with the outcome. So I continue telling my stories in my style, the only style I know, using my locations, my situations and my characters. I'll continue to submit them. Eventually someone will take notice.

NINE

The days, like thoughts, speed by
And leave me standing here.
My body sheds its youthful grace
As age approaches.

Age, with all its fears and its misgivings,
Like a menace,
Like a phantom approaches;
Looming before me
As each rising and setting of the sun
Races by with little acknowledgement of me.

How lonely is my life
When, in the stillness of my thoughts,
I look around and find
That all the world will pass me by;
That I walk only to the grave.

My pleasures and my pains
Fail to fog out the realization
That it must come;
And that when it does,
The cold earth will be my only haven;
And all my belongings will pass to another;
And before long, my name will be forgotten.

TEN

January 4th

Your parcel arrived today. It's like a late Christmas present for me. Thanks so much for the cassava pone, the coconut drops, the piece of black cake, the tooloom, the milk fudge and the sugarcakes. When I opened it, my mouth started to water. It smelled just like a Trini Christmas.

I'm especially happy for the letter. I opened it right away and have already read it twice. The first time I read it quickly, anxious to learn everything you had to say. The second time I read it slowly and aloud, trying to grasp the rhythm of your voice in every syllable.

How different we've become! My letters are cold and cumbersome while yours are free and light and full of the richness of life. Reading about all the rain before Christmas and the flood reaching right up to the back steps of the house brought back many memories.

Remember that time when the water came up so high, it was only about two feet under the big bridge? How Hollis and I and Tolo and Deo were diving off the railing, through the innertubes? And how Mr McFee's latrine started to float away, and we had to lasso it and tie it to the calabash mango tree until the flood subsided? I'm smiling now just thinking about it.

And remember the really big one the year they opened the saw mill on the junction? That time the water came up so high it covered the bridge and we had to guide the vehicles across because they couldn't tell the sides of the road. We had a good time though, carrying some of the ladies and girls across so they wouldn't get their clothes wet. Hollis must've carried you back and forth about five times that day because you kept finding excuses for Mama to send you on errands up the road... Like if she didn't know what you were up to.

Lynette's son's wedding in Carapichaima sounds grand. It's nice that they decided to hold on to the old traditions. I wish I was there to walk with everybody in the baraat from the boy's house to the girl's house accompanied all along the way by tassa drummers. I can just imagine how enjoyable it must've been. I remember Lynette from when she used to spend school holidays by Hollis and them. I didn't realize that she has children old enough to get married.

I'm really saddened though to hear about what happened to Gussy. But then, everybody always knew how dangerous his job was. Welding leaks in those giant oilfield storage tanks can spark a fire or explosion at anytime. And to think that I'd almost joined the company's apprenticeship program too. But of course, Mama wouldn't hear of it. You remember how she was so vexed with Papa and me for even considering it? She'd insisted that the jobs the apprentices trained for were too dangerous. The program created opportunities for a number of our friends though. Give Felicia and the children my condolences. I'm sure the company makes adequate provisions for the victims' families in those kinds of situations.

I'm pleased to know that you and Hollis talk to the children about me. I get much comfort from your family's happiness. Your decision to help with the scout troop is commendable. And the fact that the children are excelling in both sports and schoolwork is without doubt the result of your efforts as a hands-on mom. Your choice to quit the job to spend more time with them was a wise one. I'm happy for you. Now you have to encourage Hollis to spend more time with them too. All work and no play is not good, especially when you're raising children.

As for me, I haven't been working enough lately. The holidays really had a bad effect on me. I'm sure your letter will change that though. In fact it has already lifted my spirits and allowed me to cast off much of my depression.

ELEVEN

The very first time I ever try mih hand at writing something that I make up from mih own head was when I was in Standard Three. It was a poem about we village. Mih teacher, Miss Anna, who was from inside Mapeepee Trace, use to tell us all kinds of stories about how it was when she was a little girl growing up in the village. I use to really like to hear she stories.

    I remember how I stay up late in the night writing that poem, and how the next day, after she read it, she say she like it so much that she show it to all the other teachers in school and she make me read it for the whole class. She make me feel so proud of mih first poem that for weeks afterwards I use to walk around with it in mih bookbag, in case anybody ask to see it or to hear me read it.

    That was a long time ago. Now I don't know where it is. I can't even remember how it went. I remember though, that I start to write plenty plenty after that.

TWELVE

January 7th

Today I went for an afternoon stroll up to Times Square. I hadn't been there since the week before Christmas. Standing on the island at 46th Street where Broadway and 7th Avenue meet, I thought of the last New Year's Eve Joyce and I had spent there, six years ago.

I remembered how cold it was that night and how we'd sipped hot chocolate from a thermos and clung to each other to keep warm during the entertainment; and how we'd joined the masses of people in the loud countdown to the dropping of the ball at midnight; and how such a feeling of goodwill had prevailed, as we'd joined in hugging and kissing and wishing everyone a happy new year. The city can be such a glorious place during the holiday season when you're in the company of a loved one.

Although it's two weeks after Christmas the spirit still lingers on. The tree is still up at Rockefeller Center and people are still visiting and taking pictures and crowding against the railings captivated by the ice skaters in the rink below. The streets are still alive with shoppers and workers and tourists hurrying about.

I thought I saw someone who looked just like Teacher Toney, Samuel's father from up the road who used to teach the School Leaving class before he became a Principal down near Rio Claro. But I could've been mistaken. I was in a souvenir shop next door to the Cine 2 on Broadway looking at some t-shirts. I happened to glance outside and I saw this familiar looking face hurrying by through the crowds of people. I rushed outside but by the time I got out to the sidewalk he was gone. I looked all around but didn't see him. Well, I could've been mistaken. Or it might have been someone who looked just like him.

Afterwards I walked around for a while, but there was nothing of particular interest going on, just the usual parade of workers, window-shoppers, hawkers, tourists, exhibitionists and darting bike-messengers. After dodging around and between horn-honking taxis, revving commuter buses, commercial delivery vans and lumbering sanitation trucks, I headed down Ninth Avenue, returning home to the quiet and comfort of my apartment.

THIRTEEN

We first car was a moss-green Morris Minor Papa d'buy from a man name Bunsee in Claxton Bay for two hundred dollars. The day he bring it home, he make us dress-up in we going-out clothes, and he carry us for a spin around the village.

Man, if you d'see us! We was moving like regular big-shots, smiling and waving to all we neighbors and friends, and showing off too bad! I sure plenty people must-be well laugh at us though, because it was a real old car. The engine had a miss and the muffler had a big hole, making it sound like Mister Katwaroo tractor that d'come and grade down the hill behind the community center that same year. But to us, it was the best thing on wheels.

Every evening for a whole month afterwards, Papa use to be fixing-up that old car when he come home from work. He open-up the engine and change the rings and two lifters. Then he take down the gear box and the diff and he open them up and strip them down and clean-out all the inside parts with gas and then mount-up back everything again. Then after he put in new plugs and points and full-up fresh motor oil in the engine and gear oil in the diff, he carry it up by Dicks, the bodyworks man in Tanko Bean Trace, for him to patch and sand and paint-over the rusty spots, and weld-up the hole in the muffler.

Mama went down to San Fernando and buy some black cushion-cloth with small yellow flowers print on it, and sew-up some covers for the seats.

After a while the Morris was looking and sounding so good that Mister Bunsee couldn't believe was the same old car he d'palm-off on Papa.

On Saturdays, after Mama and Papa reach back home from the market,

Papa use to park-up the Morris in the shade under the chennet tree, and we use to wash and polish it down. On Sundays he use to pile up all of us inside the Morris and carry us to the beach or to the family cocoa land in Talparo or to visit we relatives in different parts of the island.

For three whole years the Morris take us to every nook and corner in Trinidad, till one day the engine seize-up on us when we was coming back home from Morne Diablo. Papa try everything but he couldn't get it to start back. Finally he had to pay a taxi from down there to drop us home.

A few days later he went and buy a shiny maroon Vauxhall in La Romaine, and the first thing he decide to do, was to drive down to Morne Diablo and tow the old car home. He say he just couldn't bear to leave it quite down there in some strange, lonely place it wasn't accustom to, that is why he had to go down and bring it back home.

He ask his friend Clarkie, who use to drive the papers van, to go with us, and he agree. We carry a long length of rope, and when we reach down there, we tie-up the Morris front bumper to the Vauxhall back bumper. Papa drive the Vauxhall and me and Clarkie ride in the Morris. I sit down in the back seat and Clarkie sit down in front behind the wheel to guide it and mash brakes.

When we reach home, we park-up the Morris behind the house underneath the starch mango tree, where at first, it was a part of we weekend stick-im-up games with Baalo and Coaxie and the other boys from in the street. But then after a while, when we get bigger and shift most of we games to the coconut field across the street from we house, the old Morris ended-up as a coob for Mama's setting fowls.

FOURTEEN

January 9th

I completed a draft for a new story last night. It's about a Princes Town calypsonian who, after seeking and receiving the help of a well-known Oropouche obeahman to win the Calypso Monarch competition in Port of Spain, denies the obeahman's assistance. His ingratitude and arrogance lead to a series of personal misfortunes the worst of which is a rash which breaks out all over his body. The itch is so severe that it eventually drives him insane.

This has the makings of a really interesting story because it delves into the inner workings of the calypso world and the diverse forces that are brought into play by various calypsonians and mas-people at Carnival time. Many participants in the various Carnival competitions pay quiet nighttime visits to certain priests, imams, pundits and obeahmen throughout Trinidad. It's an area of darkness and secrecy that few people in the public are aware of, but it's an active under-current to our Trini culture......

I'm writing like a maniac again. The depression I'd felt during the holidays has vanished. My whole being is once more centered on my work. When I pick up my pen, it's like opening a faucet. The words and ideas flow freely.

I'm not feeling well though. I've been coughing a lot more since last night and I have a serious headache. Dave insisted, so I'm going to see Dr Timothy, the company's doctor, tomorrow.

FIFTEEN

I am, and ever shall I be;
Though breathing fades,
Although my heart-throbs cease,
Forever shall I be.
This isn't all of me,
This mound of dirt you see.
It's but a grace, a passing time or phase;
It isn't all of me.
The weeds, the seeds, the deeds, the creeds;
The sky, the cry, the lie, the wet and dry;
They are all me, and I am they.
The trees, the breeze,
The burning and the freeze;
All birds and beasts
And tiny things that crawl;
The spheres on high,
The dragon fly,
The springtime and the fall;
I am all, and all is me.
Don't you see?
We're all the same, brother;
Inseparable;
Unable to define the boundaries of one,

The beginnings of another.
One must die to give a life,
Perhaps to neighbor, son or wife.
Maybe once I was a beast
And next I'll be somebody's niece.
For who can say from whence we came
Or whether we go to meet the same.
Never can the strength we wield
Make us masters of this field.
Within this realm we are all one;
The beast, the man, the sea, the sun.
I am you and you are I,
And never can we falsify
With word or thought or gun or knife,
The singleness of all that's life.

SIXTEEN

January 12th

I was laid-off from my job today. It came as a real shock. I'd been with the company for five and a half years and was a very good worker; never absent, never late.

Dave called me into his office and told me that there were too many complaints from other workers about my coughing. He said that Dr Timothy's report indicated that I needed rest and that the work environment was making my condition worse. It also recommended that I undergo a series of tests to determine just what is wrong with me.

I told him that I needed to work. I needed to be able to support myself. He said that I'm entitled to collect unemployment insurance for at least six months, which would provide me with a steady income and that the company would continue my medical benefits until I'm able to return to work.

Still, this is hard for me. Although I can now devote all my time to my writing, I can't help feeling used up and discarded.

SEVENTEEN

Plenty people use to say how BG Pandit was a real smartman, and how all the bhajans he does be singing and all the dhoti and kurta he wearing and the dharr he does be throwing was only a pappy-show to hide the money he was making on the side. They say how he was real money-hungry, and how he go stoop lower than a razorblade to pick up a black cent on the road.

I remember Chandarbhan, who use to work on a fishing trawler and who did stop off in British Guiana twice, saying to Papa that he feel that BG Pandit wasn't no real pandit at all. He say he feel that he wasn't even a Hindu because you does never see he or his family coming to the mandir. He say that over there, in the estate villages in BG, all the Indian people use to mix-up together and you couldn't tell who was who, and everybody use to learn one another thing, so he could just as well be a Christian or a Muslim or a plain smartman passing himself off as a pandit.

Marajin from down by the barrier say, "He cyar be no real pandit, because he too black! Only Maraj people could be pandit, and no real Maraj doh be so black!" And Parsan who does clean the mandir say, "Pandit wha'?! You ever hear bout pandit who chirren does drink rum and eat beef?!"

But BG Pandit wasn't no fool. He d'know just the right kind of answer to give when he hear that kind of talk. When he hear what Marajin say, his answer was that "God doh judge people by the color ah dey skin, only by the content ah dey heart". And as for Parsan, he say, "You does only make yuh chirren, you doh make dey mind".

He was a fast mover and a sharp talker. He was the kind of fella who was always trying something. He went up for election one time and the only reason he ent make, was because P.N.M did send up a Muslim doctor in the same district, so he get most of the Indian and the Creole votes.

A next time, he organize an interfaith committee with all the different churches in the area, but he get vex and drop out of that when they put the Presbyterian priest as chairman. He say that the whole thing was his idea and they only do that to spite him. He use to always write to the Guardian, telling them about all the religious and community works he was planning to do but they never take him on. He even went up by their office one time and carry his picture for them too, but they still ent put nothing in the papers.

Then one day, out of the blue, he get the chance he was always looking for. He was digging a yam down by the river and he notice that as he dig deeper it start taking on a distinct shape.

Oh God! His heart start to pound hard hard and a cold sweat start to run down his face because from what he could see from the top, it look like the thing start shaping-up like a man head. He could tell one time that this go be a big thing! So he start digging real real careful, using the end of his merino to clean off the dirt from it, all the while whispering to himself, "Hai Ram! Hai Ram!".

When he reach the bottom of the yam and his fingers could feel underneath it, he kneel down on his two knees and bend over the hole. Then he reach his two hands from opposite sides of the root and platt his fingers underneath it. Then jamming up the left side of his face against the side of the yam head, he start gently rocking it from side to side to loosen it from the ground. Then by slowly straightening-up his back, he lift up the whole yam from out of the hole.

When he rest it down on the ground and step back and watch, he could see for sure that it really shape just like a man head. It was about a foot high and about eight inches thick, and had a nose and mouth and eyes just like a man head.

But the thing that really ketch him was how the shape of the head and the face and everything about it make it look just like the Lord Krishna picture in the New Years almanac he did get from Deluxe store in San Fernando.

"Hai Ram! Hai Ram!" he kept whispering to himself. He start sweating cold cold cold. His head start to spin. His belly start to gripe. He feel like he go faint away. He had to hold on to a fig tree for support till his head clear-up.

When he catch himself, and he realize that this was the thing he was waiting all these years for, he pick up that yam root and start running up the road like a madman, bawling out hard hard how God give him a sign, and how the head was Lord Krishna. He was making so much ruckshun that people start running out of their houses to hear what the commotion was about.

Hugging-up the yam against his chest, he kept gasping to everyone he pass, "Look, Lord Krishna….Lord Krishna head!"

Well, you know how we Trinis stop already. We ent letting nothing pass we straight. Any chance for a bacchanal or a sensation Trinis always right there. In no time at all, a whole procession form all around him, following and trying to catch a glimpse of the Lord Krishna head. But he keep hugging it up against his chest close close so nobody can't get a good view.

When he reach home he carry the yam straight inside the house. He make his wife tie up the front gate and let go the two pot-hounds, so nobody can't come in the yard. Then he gone by the wares-stand and quick, quick, he take a handful of coconut fiber and some ashes and scrub out all the dirt from the yam. Then he rinse it out with fresh water and rub it down with ghee, and put it in a tariah that he make his wife manjay till it was shining like new. He make his grand-children pick some fencing flowers and make a mala for around the neck and a pahgree for on top the head and he light some deyas and put around it on the tariah. Then he bathe and put on a clean dhoti and kurta.

Well all this time word was spreading like lightning. People start coming down to see. In no time at all it look like if was joovay-morning High Street outside; big, big traffic jam from quite up the road. When BG Pandit see what was happening his heart start to beat fast, fast and his brains start to work like the cat-cracker.

Meantime Dolphus, the Guardian reporter from up inside Boncane, hear what was going on, so he grab his camera, his pen and his notebook and jump in his car and race down there. When he reach and see crowd so, he stop the car in the middle of the road, scramble outside and start snapping pictures one time.

All this time BG Pandit have his gate close up so everybody gather-up in the road outside, shouting for him to show them the Lord Krishna head. Nobody ent going near the gate though, because he have his two black-mouth pot-hounds let-go and running around in the yard.

For more than two hours he sit down inside trying to figure out his next move while the crowd outside keep growing bigger and bigger and noisier and noisier. Then he spot Dolphus outside snapping pictures with his camera, talking to people and scribbling in his notebook.

BG Pandit get up one time and walk out in the gallery and raise-up his hands to quiet down the crowd. Then he shout out so that everybody could hear, especially Dolphus. "When I dig up Lord Krishna today, I hear a voice inside mih head, talking to me. It say, 'Pandit, I giving you a sign dat everybody could see, and I want you to give dis message to all d'people. Tell dem dat I am real real disappointed dat up to now Lord Krishna eh have no proper home in dis part ah Trinidad. Tell dem dat I say dat dey must do everything in dey power t'provide a proper home arong here for Lord Krishna; and dat I want it to be here in dis village; and tell dem dat is why I choose you today t'help dem provide dat home, by collectin' funds t'build a kutya in yuh front yard for Lord Krishna'."

Then he pause for a moment to let that sink in and then he continue, "So all who want t'see d'sign wha' I geh today, g'have t'make a contribution for we to build a Lord Krishna kutya before you could come inside."

Just that day alone he must be collect about four hundred dollars. The next day it come out in the papers with one of the pictures that Dolphus take.

Well if yuh see thing! People start coming from all over Trinidad to see the Lord Krishna head, and BG Pandit doing real business. Day and night they coming. Little children and big people; Hindu, Christian and Muslim; Chinee, Indian and Creole; even some white people from the oilfield come and all. Everybody coming to see the miracle, and BG Pandit collecting money like crazy!

And not only that! When they start seeing people so, his wife start selling doubles and saheena and poolowrie and fry channa, and his children and grandchildren start selling sweet drink and mauby and snow cone.

For about three weeks it gone on just so, and then just as it start, it stop. Somebody up in Caroni had a cattle that make a young one with one eye in the middle of the forehead, and although it born peenee peenee, like if it have marazmee, people start rushing up there to see that miracle. They forget all about BG Pandit and his Lord Krishna head. By that time though, he d'done collect a good few thousand dollars.

Well after about three months pass, we start to wonder whether BG Pandit was really going to build this kutya for Lord Krishna. At first everybody thought that he was going to start building it because we notice that he buy up gravel and sand and red bricks and cement and stack it up near his house and then he hire Dadaboy the Grenadian to do the work. But then, after a while, we notice that Dadaboy wasn't building no kutya. Instead he take the material and start building over BG Pandit house.

Well you know how Trinis stop already. All the big people start puss-pussing and scheupsing and cussing among themselves. Some of them saying he's a darm thief. Some of them saying he's a smartman. Some of them saying they should jail him and throw away the key. Some of them saying they should give him a good cut-ass. But nobody ent want to come out to his face and ask him about the kutya, till somebody gone easy and complain to the Guardian.

So the Guardian send back Dolphus to ask him, "Way the kutya?" How come he building over his house, when he d'say, and they have it quote right there in the papers, that God d'speak to him and tell him to build a kutya in his front yard for the Lord Krishna. So way the kutya, Pandit?.... Way the kutya!?

Well, cool as cucumber, BG Pandit explain to Dolphus, and this was in the papers the next day, that all he was doing was following new instructions from God.

He say that God d'talk to him again in a dream one night....You remember about two months ago, he tell Dolphus, when it had heavy heavy rain and bright bright lightning and hard hard thunder whole day and whole night?....Well that night God d'talk to him again and tell him, "Pandit, judgin' from d'kinda weather all yuh havin' in Trinidad dese days, d'Lord Krishna really shouldn' be outside in no choonky, lil kutya, facin' d'wind and rain and lightnin' and thunder, while you and yuh whole family well cover-up from head to toe with nice nice cotton ched-darr and sleepin' comfortable inside d'house. So I think d'right thing is fuh you t'make yuh whole house a kutya for d'Lord Krishna, yes." He say that is why he building over his house, so that instead of it being just any regular old house, the whole thing go be a kutya for the Lord Krishna.

This cause Marajin to tell Parsan, "You eh see? D'darm man feel he's Lord Krishna now. He buildin' kutya for heself!" To which Parsan reply, "Good ting he eh ketch me. Why you tink me ent give 'im one red cent. I sure dat he eh go be usin' none ah my blood and sweat money to do it!"

EIGHTEEN

January 16th

I've been out of work for four days now and I still can't get used to it. I get dressed every single morning and go out and walk around for about an hour before returning to my room.

The cough has become much more persistent. It's dry and painful and I have no control over it. Sometimes I see little specks of blood in my saliva. The headaches bother me the most though. It's not the usual headaches I used to get.

Now when they strike, I feel my whole head throbbing. They come on suddenly, last for about half an hour and then go away. There's no warning before they come or go. Dr. Timothy has made an appointment for me to have a series of tests at Bellevue Hospital on the 19th, only a few days away. We'll see.

I've started work on my novel again. It's set in a remote south coast fishing village which I call Manicou Bay, and tells the story of my main character Cutty, the middle-aged, one-legged caretaker of the village boatshed.

My story is told in the form of a conversation between Cutty and a young anthropology student from England. He's studying at UWI and is spending a few days, camping on the beach in Manicou Bay, doing research for his thesis *'The Ocean in the Life of the People of Trinidad & Tobago'*. He claims to be the son of a Trinidadian mother, who migrated to England while he was still a child.

The conversation takes place one night at the boatshed after the usual night lime has broken up and all the men have gone home. The young man is probing with his questions and Cutty, loosened by the effects of the puncheon rum he'd been drinking with the other men, is forthcoming.

He relates how, as a young man in central Trinidad, he was a school teacher; how fresh out of the Government Teacher's Training College, with a wife and a five month old baby son to support, he'd been called to join the British Commonwealth forces fighting the Nazis in Europe; how it felt to leave little Trinidad to go and join the big war, to kill in the line of duty, to have his left leg blown off by a landmine, and to be captured and spend time as a prisoner of War in a German hospital; how he returned home after the war, as a decorated hero, and for his sacrifice, was rewarded with the post of Assistant Principal at a government elementary school in a suburb of Port of Spain; and how after only three years, just when it seemed that he'd settled back into a normal life, memories of the horrors of the war, the guilt for the lives he'd taken, the terror of his capture, the pain from his injuries and the insecurities caused by his one-leggedness, came back to haunt him; how his wife had grown impatient with his endless nightmares, his frequent rantings and his destructive temper tantrums which were scaring his son away from him; how he sought refuge in the company of an old girlfriend from his high school days, who now ran a rum-shop near the market on Charlotte Street, where he would sit for hours recounting his experiences to her and to anyone else who would listen; how one night a fight at the rum-shop led to another man's death at his hands; how he was arrested and charged with murder; how, although he was acquitted in the case because witnesses testified that he'd acted in self-defense, his wife, claiming that he'd shamed her, took the child and left the country, and the Ministry forced him to resign his job; how disgraced, he'd left Trinidad on a windjammer, working his way up and down the islands of the Eastern Caribbean; then how, after fourteen years at sea, he'd returned to Trinidad and settled quietly in Manicou Bay, far from the bustle of Port of Spain, where he now lived alone next to the boatshed, in a shack overlooking the ocean.

Here, living anonymously, he'd found some measure of peace. Here he'd rise before dawn everyday to blow the conch shell, to awaken the boatmen.

Then he'd brew a pot of double-strength coffee, sweetened with condensed milk, in time for them before they caught the first waves out. The rest of his day he spent mending nets, caulking boats, pulling seine and making a pitch-oil tin of fish broth for the usual evening lime at the boatshed, where most of the men would gather to play all-fours, drink puncheon and old-talk while they cleaned their boats and serviced the engines in preparation for the next day's work.

Within the confines of this story I've been reaching back into my own thoughts and feelings and experiences to flesh out the characters and the situations.

As the story unfolds the young man begins to sense some parallels between what Cutty was relating and his own story because he'd also been separated from his father since early childhood, when his mother had taken him and migrated to England…

My only problem is that it's an emotionally exhausting exercise and every time I'd worked on it before, I'd found it difficult to stay with it for long. This time however I intend to persevere until it's completed.

NINETEEN

Unlike the floating cloud that floats
Unlike the singing bird that sings
Unlike the falling rain that falls
I think and plan
And pour my life
In how I should
And not in doing.

TWENTY

January 19th

I spent the whole day today at Bellevue Hospital. My appointment was at 8:30 this morning and I didn't get back home until just after six o'clock, about half an hour ago. The waiting for everything was so long!

They took a series of X-rays then they started testing. They took a blood test and a saliva test and a stool test and a urine test. Then they checked for typhoid and TB and syphilis, and cancer and diabetes and hepatitis, lymphoma and hepatoma and leukemia, melanoma and bulimia and pneumonia; and on and on and on…

After hours and hours of looking and chooking, and pounding and sounding, and prying and spying at every nook and cranny of my body; and after questioning me about my life history, my family history, my ancestral history and my travel history; about my eating habits, my social habits, my work habits and my sexual habits they sent me home with no answers, and feeling sicker and more confused than when I first got there.

All they gave me before I left were some tablets for the headache and the fever, a bottle of syrup for the cough and another appointment for the 23rd of this month.

TWENTY ONE

A thin gray stream of smoke
Drifts upward from the tip,
Which, glowing between my fingers,
Casts an eerie light
Of ghosts and faded images of old;
Images that have, for some time now,
Brought back to mind,
The streets where all my heaven once lay.

Yea, as a child,
Those very streets of wind-ball cricket fields
And pitching marble arenas
Did seem to hold the pulse of life;
For it was there, with lusty youth,
We'd played and pranked and fought;
And in the night,
Stole kisses from the careless misses
Who, with questionable innocence,
Had dared to wander in the shadows
Near the fences and the stairs.
It was upon those streets
That I first gazed
Into the mysteries of my body and my mind.
They were the length and breadth of all my world.

The faces of the folks who came and went
All seemed to bear a legend each its own.

Days and weeks and months and years
Would come and go
And still my streets remained unchanged,
Though some among us died
And some were born
And some were wed
And some would move away,
My streets remained unchanged.
But now it's not the same....
As if by sudden force of some great tyrant's hand
Or Nature's sometimes cold and heartless creed,
They've all now disappeared.
The lightening claws of fate have stricken,
All at once it seems,
The sights and sounds and faces of my youth.
Where is the laughter and the fun of yesterday?
No more do old men walk the streets at night
Delighting youth with tales of former times.
No more, with boisterous mirth, do children play,
Devouring each moment of an August night.
It seems a dream now.
The sidewalks reek with torment and with sin.
Where once these streets had throbbed
With sights and smells and sounds of all humanity;
Where once the displaced pilgrims came
From distant shores in flocks and droves,
Bringing with them a culture each his own;
Where once these streets had welcomed
The frightened souls of all who'd fled here,

*In search of what they could not elsewhere find,
There's nothing now
But pain and fear and desperation.*

*I am not man enough to weep
When, in the prison of my mind,
I find myself alone, devoid of joy or hope,
Untouched, unloved, uncared for
By this life of false, pretentious smiles.
I sit here by my window
And contemplate with heavy heart
The differences from then to now.
Sometimes I walk the streets
Where as a child I'd played.
Another group now plays another game.
Has it all really changed?
Or is it that my eyes no longer see
What, as a child, they did?*

TWENTY TWO

January 25th

My novel is now galloping along at a hectic pace. It's flinging open secret doors to wildly divergent, emotional chambers deep inside of me. My mind is in a constant daze, existing only within the realm of my story. It occupies my every waking moment; sometimes even my dreams.

Images long forgotten; images that had flickered through my thoughts then disappeared are now returning, flooding my memory, tapping new springs of insight, adding new dimensions to my characters.

My mind is on fire! A vast new world has burst open inside me! I slip easily into this world of my characters. I see them and touch them and listen to them as their stories unfold. I nudge them in this direction or push them into that situation and allow them to react. It's a truly exhilarating sensation. I'm young and alive again!

It reminds me of how I used to feel when, as a college student in San Fernando, I would rush out of school at lunch time and head for New or Radio City or Strand or Gaiety on Mucurapo Street and pay the checker six cents to catch the last half hour of the 10 a.m. double feature. We used to call it "Six Cents Reel" in those days.

Every time I entered one of those dark, hot, sweaty, smelly cinemas, it was like walking into my own private paradise. For those thirty to forty minutes every day, I'd allow myself to be absorbed into the lives, the customs and the intrigues of a vast array of people, from a vast array of cultures, inhabiting a vast array of locales; from The Bay of Bengal to The OK Corral; from The Streets of Laredo to The Snows of Kilimanjaro;

from East of Sumatra to West of Zanzibar; from the Harbor Lights to the Wuthering Heights; from The Mutiny on The Bounty to A Town Without Pity.

It was there in the darkness of those Mucurapo Street movie houses that I first became aware of the wild cavalcade of ideas bombarding my youthful brain; that I first began to recognize the breadth, depth and infinity of my imagination; and that I first dared to dream of the possibility of creating fantasies of my own…

Right now in my novel, I have Cutty in a flashback to the moment in the war when he's faced with taking a life for the first time. He's crouched inside a foxhole, on a hill overlooking a country road, his rifle trained on an enemy soldier manning a machine gun halfway down the hill, waiting in ambush for an approaching jeep carrying two British officers. With only seconds to act, Cutty breaks into a cold sweat. His body begins to tremble.

He recalls how as a boy one New Years, he'd helped his father and his uncle kill a goat for the holiday. They were doing the killing. He just had to help by holding on to the back legs to prevent it from kicking-up too much. The animal's anguished cries and the look of horror in its eyes almost caused him to faint. He could never forget the blood squirting from the fresh gash on its neck and its desperate struggle, at first violent, then slowly ebbing into a twitching and a shuddering and a trembling, as the life seeped out of its muscles. He'd felt the fading energy pass through his hands and through his shoulders and throughout his entire body as it drifted away. He was so traumatized by the experience he could never even harm a chicken after that.

This however, was not a goat or a chicken his rifle was aimed at. This was another human being; probably with a wife and a child at home, just like him. If he shoots, would he be able to justify it in his own mind? Then again, if he didn't act now, this enemy soldier waiting in ambush would certainly blow away his two unsuspecting colleagues. He couldn't allow that to happen, for he was a soldier.

Here, in the Royal Army, he'd been taught that he must either kill or be killed. There was no in-between. There was no time for emotions or analyses. No time for excuses. No time for hesitation. This was war. There must be no thought of right or wrong here, only duty.

As the jeep rounds the corner, Cutty snaps out of his reverie and pulls the trigger...

I went back to Bellevue Hospital the day before yesterday for my second appointment. They said that the results were inconclusive but because they found that I was severely anemic, they wanted to ward me for a few days to build me up before running further tests. They said that they were troubled by what appeared to be an imbalance in the components of my blood. I have no idea what that means, and the doctors wouldn't explain further. They just kept up the same old mantra about me staying in the hospital and running more tests.

Well I don't intend to be anybody's guinea pig, so I refused. They tried to convince me, but I wouldn't give in, so they took some more blood for further testing, gave me more medication and allowed me to go home.

TWENTY THREE

Me and Davey get a jackass one time from a fella name Hookey in Palmyra. It was a nice jackass yes, but Hookey say that though the jackass use to work good, he get darm fed up with it, because anytime it see a heap of fresh sand, it leaving all work and everything and going to roll and play in the sand. And it wasn't interested in no old, dry-up, bind-up, hard hard heap of sand either. Is only fresh, loose, still wettish sand that use to send this jackass bazodee.

The day Hookey finally decide to get rid of the jackass, he was coming down a big hill on the main road near his carat house in Palmyra, riding on the cart, load-up with a big big load of canetop. Down at the bottom of the hill was a fresh heap of red-sand the road-works people d'drop that morning to start building a new concrete drain next day.

The jackass was coasting along, cool and calm and lazy as usual, when in the distance he spot the sand-heap. Well, he stop dead in his tracks. Then he cock up his tail, start to bray, take off full speed down the hill and dive straight into the sand-heap. Hookey and the cart full of canetop and everything gone flying in the drain while the jackass braying hard hard and rolling around in the sand.

Boiling mad, Hookey pull himself out of the drain, covered from head to toe in stink, black mud and after cussing up the jackass and cracking him some heavy blows with a length of bobbon cane, he decide there and then that he didn't want this jackass no more. This jackass was just too much trouble for him!

It so happen that me and Davey was passing right there on a hike from Corosan at the same time and although he didn't know us, he offer us the jackass because he just wanted to get rid of it and we agree one time to take it.

Well right away we start to feel like if we was Lone Ranger and Tonto self. We ride the jackass from Palmyra all the way home; two of us on top the jackass back one time. We gone through canefield and cornfield, and rozopatch and lashpatch, and paragrass and bullgrass and ploughland and breakland. We even make it swim over the river with the two of us on top the back.

Now, we couldn't let we parents know that we have this jackass, so we carry it in the bush in Ghobarrland and tie it out, and we start going down there every day and acting like if we was cowboys out on the open western range, riding the jackass all over Ghobarrland.

And we start behaving like if we was real cowboys too, calling one another Ringo and Jesse. We even start dressing up to look like cowboys with two old hats on we heads which we curl-up on the sides to look like cowboy hats; and wearing gun-belts with holster and caps-guns around we waists; and tying kerchiefs around we necks; and walking bandy-leg like James Whitmore we favorite actor in cowboy movies; and having gunfights every day, crawling on we bellies between the mosquito and kozay-mahoe bushes; and ducking for cover behind the mammey-sepote and baraharr trees.

And if you hear how we talking! The two of us develop a twang like if we come-out straight from Texas, using words like 'pardner' and 'coyotee' and 'buzzard' and 'sidewinder'. We gone so far as to take a set of dry-up corn grass and ball it up in two big big balls, high almost up to we chest and tie them up inside some old mosquito netting so they ent go fall apart and start rolling them around and calling them tumbleweed.

We even start making a raise from the jackass too, because all the young fellas in the area want a ride, so we take a piece of old plank and make up a sign mark "OK CORRAL" and start charging. It was five cents for a plain ride four times around the wind-ball cricket field; and ten cents if you want to shoot me or Davey dress up as an Apache while you riding the jackass; and fifteen cents if you want to make a pappyshow of yuhself by having me or Davey shoot you off the jackass back at the end of yuh ride, so you could fall in the patch of bull-grass near the kayan guava tree and tumble all the way down the hill to the drain by the tiger-wire fence.

Things was going real good for about a whole month. News start to spread about the gunfights at the OK CORRAL and fellas start showing-up from all up Mayo and Sum Sum Hill and Piparo. Me and Davey was doing so good that we was sure we go get rich from this venture in no time at all. We never dream that anything could ever go wrong, until one fo-day morning the jackass getaway and gone in Chandroo garden.

When day clear and Chandroo gone in his garden, he spot mister jackass, cool and calm as you please, eating peas trees left and right. Pardners, well Chandroo gone crazy! And when you see Chandroo gone crazy, everybody does know about it.

He start to cuss and get-on one time! Man, the whole village could hear him. In fact, the whole village make it their business to come out and see him in action; because Chandroo wasn't no ordinary cuss-bud. He never use to cuss often like Sylvie and Rooplal and them, because he use to spend most of his time alone in his garden, but when you see an occasion come up and he let loose, nobody couldn't match him. Chandroo was a man use to put flair and flamboyance into his cussing. He was like a calypsonian of cuss. And this morning he was in tip-top form.

If you see him coming down the road! He have the jackass rope tie around his waist and he holding-up, over his head, a set of peas trees in his left hand and his cutlass in his right hand. And he speechifying like the Midnight Robber on Carnival day, telling the story about how he weed up the land and he fork up the land, and he spray down the land to kill all the bugs and mites and parasites; and how he rich-up the soil with plenty plenty urea and plenty plenty manure; and how he kneel down on his two knees in the hot hot sun and he make long long beds in the ground; and how he went by the agriculture place in San Fernando by the top of St. James Street and buy up the best peas seeds you ever see; and how he wait till full moon come and he plant them seeds in the name of the Lord; and how he water them morning, noon and night; and how he mold them up every day; and pull out the weeds as soon as they show their heads; and how he watch them peas plants grow up big big and strong strong and healthy healthy; and how all his trees was full up now with nice nice, fat fat peas.

Then he start to sing a calypso that he was making up right there on the spot, about how planting is the Lord work and destroying is the devil work; and how jump high or jump low, the Lord go always conquer the devil.

But the thing that put Chandroo in a class by himself was that he was a fella use to act out everything. And he was a real good actor too; striking all kinds of poses and twisting up his body and his face in all kinds of strange, strange expressions.

And then on top of that, this wasn't no slow slow, dead dead calypso he was singing neither. This was a road-march tempo calypso. This was a dance and jump-up calypso.

So along with the speechifying and the calypso singing and the dramatic posing he was also jumping-up in the air and wining-up his bamsee and rolling on the ground and swiping his cutlass 'Shwyye! Shwyye!' on the road. So he bawling and laughing and singing and crying long long tears all at the same time. But mostly he was cussing.

The whole speech was mainly cuss. Even with the Lord name he cussing; all kinds of cuss; regular, everyday cuss and cuss you never dream about before. Chandroo was a fella coulda take ordinary ordinary words and turn them to real real believable cuss. He coulda take simple game names like goes-in goes-out and lerr-kee, and fruit names like sapodilla and mamey-sepote and gommishel fig, and vegetable names like tomatoes and bygan and cucumber and give them all kinds of nasty meanings different different to what they really mean.

He take more than an hour and a half to haul the jackass the quarter mile from his garden in Ghobarrland down to the police station pound.

When me and Davey hear what happen, we realize one time that we was in big big trouble. We figure that Chandroo didn't know yet who jackass it was, but that if he find out, he go make sure that the police lock us up and make we parents pay for all the peas trees that the jackass eat; and that go mean some real big trouble for us at home. So we sit down and make out a plan.

That evening we make a hand-barrow with two bamboo poles and a half sheet of galvanize. Then we wait till after midnight when everybody was sleeping and we take the hand-barrow and a shovel and gone up by Ellen Street junction where Mr. De Freitas d'bring plenty material to build a new concrete house. Making sure that we ent make no noise, we load up the hand-barrow with sand from the sand-heap and head back down the road to the back of the police station.

When we reach there we see the jackass tie up inside the stable and Constable Theophilus sitting down on a chair outside the stable door, sleeping with his head sideways on his shoulder, and snoring loud loud, with his mouth wide open and his big belly jiggling like a basin full of sago pap every time he exhale.

Me and Davey creep up behind a bush near the stable door and put down the hand barrow with the sand on the ground. Then Davey take up a handful of sand and pelt it but it land right outside the stable door. The jackass just raise-up his head and sniff and snort a couple of times but ent do nothing else, so Davey take up a next handful and angle himself properly. Taking a good aim he pelt the next handful and it fly straight inside the stable door. This time the jackass was just turning to face the door when the handful of fresh, red sand catch him straight in the face.

Pardners, well like jumbie take him! He start to jump up and down, pelting back-kicks at the stable door and braying Hee Hawh!! Hee Hawh!! hard-hard-hard. Constable Theophilus jump up from his chair, dotish with sleep, and run by the stable door just as the jackass burst his rope. With one solid back-kick the jackass fling the stable door wide open, knocking down Constable Theophilus to the ground.

Me and Davey grab up the barrow of sand and start running. The jackass take-off full speed behind us, still braying hard-hard. We was making so much noise that people start to wake up in the village as we race towards the river. We run all the way down the road till the jackass catch up with us near by Miss Jaynee pudden stall. We drop the barrow of sand on the ground just as the jackass dive in and start rolling around.

Me and Davey let him play in the sand for a few minutes but then we grab the rope and drag him away because we could hear Constable Theophilus blowing hard, hard, pedaling his bike, coming down the road towards us.

We swim the jackass over the river and cut across the canefield before taking the taska road behind the weighing crane to the next side of the teak plantation. Then we follow the new concrete drain to Hookey's karat-house in Palmyra. We bang and bang and bang on the door till Hookey and his wife wake up and light a flambeau and open the door.

When Hookey see me and Davey standing there with the jackass, he was vex like hell that we come waking up he and his wife two o'clock in the morning and he cuss us up because he say that we ent have no consideration for a hard working man who does be breaking his balls for the whole day and could only catch a few hours sleep in the nighttime.

When we tell him that we bring back the jackass, well is then he get mad! He start to cuss hard hard. He say that he didn't want back no darm jackass; that this jackass done cause too much trouble for him already; that is why he give us it in the first place; that the jackass was we own now; and that if we know what good for us, we better take the so and so jackass and get off his property now, and we better don't wake him up again, cause the next time he open his door, he go have his poo-yah in his hand; and he left us with that and gone back inside and slam the door in we face.

Well, we could tell that Hookey mean business and that we couldn't fool around with him, but we know too, that we couldn't take a chance and carry the jackass back with us either, because we didn't want Chandroo or the police or we parents to link the jackass to us, so we turn around and pretend that we was leaving with the jackass.

Instead we hide in the bush behind Hookey house till we hear him snoring again and was sure that he gone back to sleep. Then, making sure that we didn't make no noise, we creep up and tie the jackass on a post on the side of the house. After petting the animal a few times to mamaguy it so that it eh go make no noise, we leave it there and crawl through the bullgrass till we reach the new concrete drain; then we take off full speed down the drain and ent slow down again till we reach the teak plantation.

From there we walk back around the weighing crane, up the taska road and through the canefield. Then we swim over the river and reach back home just when cock start crowing and the day was starting to clear.

TWENTY FOUR

February 1st

The new medications have done wonders for me. I feel free again. My spirits are up, my juices are flowing, my mind is on the move. Work on my novel has become a source of constant delight. It's a never ending high. The world outside seems distant and boring now. I live in a new world. This world which flows from the tip of my pen is one of deep passion and constant excitement!

Thanks for the newspapers. I see that Carnival season is in full swing again. I got home-sick just reading about the excitement of the season back home, and reminiscing about the designers, wire-benders and mas-players at the mas-camps; the drummers, chanters and boismen at the gayals; the calypsonians, musicians and comedians at the calypso tents and the tuners, arrangers and players at the panyards, all working and practicing for the big celebration. This led me in my novel, to place Cutty at Invaders pan-yard on Tragarete Road....

It's the evening when he first makes up his mind to visit Rosalie at her rumshop on Charlotte Street. He'd been feeling more and more isolated at home. His wife Mandy had grown distant. His son was spending too much of his time with his Uncle Teddy. And Mandy's sister Beulah was openly hostile towards him.

The atmosphere at the pan-yard, the excitement of the tuners working on the instruments, the arranger drilling each player in particular runs, the supporters soaking-in the energy for release on the two days of Carnival, and the players coming together to create this irresistible music, was a comfort to him; particularly today.

For today was especially troubling. Today he'd learned that his sister-in-law Beulah and her husband Teddy were planning to migrate to England and were encouraging Mandy to take his son and make the move with them. He'd panicked. He had to talk to someone. He needed to pour out his feelings and his fears to someone and ever since he'd run into his old friend Rosalie in the Savannah last month and she'd greeted him so warmly and asked him to come by, he'd toyed with the thought. When practice ended and everyone was leaving the yard, he took a Round-d-Town taxi and headed for Rosalie's rumshop on Charlotte Street...

So how is your Carnival shaping up? Are you and Hollis taking the kids to Port of Spain this year or back to San Fernando?

Remember how Mama and Papa used to take us to 'our spot' at the Library corner; Papa and I carrying the benches, and you and Mama carrying the handbags with the eats and drinks? We used to have so much fun! Especially when some of Papa's work friends who were playing 'Jab Jab' or 'Pay d Devil' or 'Wild Indian' would come and dance-up in front of us and threaten to throw powder or rub grease on us; and we'd scream and run through the crowds with them jokingly chasing after us; and then, when they'd flop down on the pavement to rest by us, they'd let us try on their headpieces or play with their whips and lances. It was a glorious time for us then!

I think that you and Hollis should start involving the children in carnival. They can begin by participating in the kiddy's carnival at Skinner's Park. You should also consider having them learn to play the pan. It's our instrument you know. When you live away from home you begin to realize how much your own culture means to you.

TWENTY FIVE

A sound synonymous with home;
Like the tune of bees a-humming;
Like so many guitars strumming;
A pedestal with a lighted dome.

From discarded barrels of oil,
For a joyous and rhythmic sound,
Echoing through village and town,
With my hammer and chisel I toil.

TWENTY SIX

February 6th

To me society has become shallow and insignificant. Sitting here by my window every day, watching people hurrying to or from their jobs, I can't help wondering why it's considered so necessary.

Why must we toil away each day in a factory or an office, doing someone else's bidding for a few dollars, which seldom brings us satisfaction anyway? From whence came this misguided ambition, that forces us into lives of constant servitude?

Right now I consider myself lucky to be sitting here in the security of my room, surveying the aimlessness of the world outside; lucky to have been pushed off the constantly revolving roller coaster of life's trivial responsibilities; lucky to have been taught finally that no one is indispensable; that we're only duped into feeling that we are.

I used to think that my input was necessary and that certain wheels would grind to a halt if I should suddenly withdraw. Since my lay-off from the company I've learned differently.

I've finally come to realize that I was merely a tool, performing for the benefit and the delight of others.

Why should I ease another's burdens while ignoring the turmoil within my own breast?

TWENTY SEVEN

The old people use to say that the river was haunted. They say that where we village is now, use to be a Carib burial ground, and the spirits of the old-time Warahoons was still roaming the river. They say how an Arawak lady baby d'drown there and she had put a curse on the river before throwing she self in the water and drowning too, just like she baby; and that sometimes in the night you could hear the baby crying and the mother moaning in the bamboo patch along the river bank.

We use to try not to take them on when they say so, because we use to think that they saying it just to frighten us from swimming by we selves in the river. But they use to always insist that the river must take at least one life from around we village every year; so whenever anybody drown, you was sure to hear them whispering, "Is the curse."

The river was important to everybody who grow up in we village. Is in the river where we learn to swim and catch fish. Is in the river where Fyzool and them use to throw away the hosay every year, and all we boys use to dive in and try to get the moon and star from the top.

Dougla Sheppy use to plant garden near by the river and during corn-season when Saturday morning come and we see him load-up his jitney and gone to sell in the market, me and Coaxie use to head down to his corn-field to thief corn and boil it in a butter pan right there on the riverbank, using water from the river.

The sweetest experiment cane and the greenest para grass use to grow down by the river.

The football ground is right by the river too, and every evening when we done practice, we use to go in the river for a dip, to wash out the rotten mud from we skin.

We parents teach us to swim in the river, and then use to blows us when we go down there by we selves.

We use to get the tallest and straightest bamboo rods from the bamboo patch by the river whenever we going over the wire to chook down coconuts in the estate lands.

Young couples use to hide and meet by the river, and the Baptist people use to do their blessings down by the river.

Me and Ralph d'take a rowboat from the estate dam one Sunday and drag it about a hundred yards through the coconut, and a next hundred yards through the tall bull grass, down to the river, and spend the whole day in the river playing Davey Crockett, King of the Wild Frontier, with we friends from the street. Next day the estate police catch Bugsy and them from up in Lime Trace laughing hard hard and rowing the boat up and down the river. All of them lose their yard-boy work in the estate because of that.

A next time Choko nearly burn down the whole village when he set fire by accident in a stretch of dry corn-grass near the river while roasting a ground-dove. He try to out it by himself, but the wind was too strong and the fire get away and jump in the bamboo patch. All of us run down to help, but we couldn't manage. Flames was shooting high high up in the air. Fire brigade had to come from quite San Fernando to out it. Choko get so much blows from his father for that, he couldn't sit down comfortable for a whole week after that.

If a child missing, the first place they use to start looking was down by the river, and if somebody see jumbie you could bet yuh life is down by the river they see it.

Yes, the old people use to always tell us about the curse on the river and we use to just laugh and pass it off as old talk. But one thing was sure sure sure, a whole year could never pass by without we village or the surrounding area losing at least one life to the river.

TWENTY EIGHT

February 9th

I went out today. I was feeling lonely and homesick and because the weather isn't too bad, I decided to get out and take the subway down to Brooklyn and visit some of the shops on Nostrand Avenue. I hadn't been there for over a year.

It was such a comfort to fill my ears with the lilt of Caribbean accents and catch the scent of coconut drops and currants rolls and fresh hops bread.

Standing on Fulton Street, eating a chicken roti, watching the constant flow of people and listening to the latest calypsos blasting from inside Charlie's record shop, made me think of Joyce and the time we had stood on the sidewalk outside of Madison Square Garden watching a large crowd of New Yorkers grooving to the sounds of a lone steelpan player from down home.

That was exactly one year after she'd left her family to come and live with me so it was like an anniversary celebration for us. She'd told me that she'd never felt so proud of our country and our culture as she did on that day. Before I left Brooklyn, I bought a container of cow heel soup from Mara's on Nostrand to bring back home to my room. I'm having it tonight before I go to bed.

TWENTY NINE

It had a time in Trinidad when hitch-hiking was the craze. No matter where we going we use to try to mop a ride. Sometimes just for fun we use to divide up in groups and race around the island mopping rides.

We use to start-off by walking out to the main road junction; then we'd mop a ride heading north through Chaguanas to the corner of Princess Margaret and Churchill Roosevelt Highway; then east through Tunapuna and Arima to Sangre Grande; then south along the Manzanilla stretch to Mayaro; then west through Rio Claro and Princess Town before we get back home; and we riding anything that stop for us; truck, car, van, bike, donkey-cart, tractor, anything.

All kinds of people use to stop for us too! One time me and Tan Tan went for oysters in Monkey Point. When we finish and we leave the mangrove and start walking back home on the main road, we see this big, fancy, black car driving up from a distance. Just for joke we put out we hands as the car was speeding by, and to we surprise, the car stop. But that was joke surprise! The real surprise for we was when we run up to the car and gone by the window to explain that we was only joking. Is then we notice that the driver was an important and popular government minister whose picture use to be in the papers almost every day.

He ask us where we was going and when we tell him, he say he was going to give a speech at a function in Oropouche, and he could give us a drop in Marabella by the roundabout. We tell him that is awright, we go walk. But he say he was glad for the company. Even when we show him that we clothes was soaking wet, he still say is no problem because the car seats had plastic covers.

He was a real nice person. I sit down in front with him, and Tan Tan sit down in the back, and we talk whole road. Well, was really he who talk. We mostly listen.

He say that sometimes he wish he was young again so he could do what we was doing. He talk right through from the time he pick us up until he drop us off in Marabella. In that short space of time he talk about crime and politics and problems in the country and how people have to care more for one another and for their family and for the country as a whole. He say that there should be more recreation for young people so they don't have to get in so much trouble like was the trend nowadays.

I don't know if he d'just like to talk or if he was practicing his speech on us that he was going to give at the function in Oropouche that evening. He was a real nice man though and after that I used to check the papers everyday to read anything they write about him.

It wasn't always easy on the road though. Sometimes we use to get rag-up too bad! Like the time the island come up in Chatham and me and Shah and Bolo decide to go down and check it out. Well, rides was hard like hell to get down that side and we had to walk most of the way in the hot hot sun. After we pass the sharp corner down by Cap-de-ville we see an old truck coming up the road with a cow in the tray; so we start waving and shouting to the driver to stop. He pass us straight but when he reach about fifty yards down the road, he shift to second gear and start to slow down. Talk about run! Man we take off full speed behind the truck, happy like hell to get a ride at last, but when we nearly reach, the driver push out his head from the window and shout out, "Way yuh wawh mih t'put all yuh!? In d'cow kakahole!?" And with that he start laughing hard hard hard, as he step on the gas and drive away.

A next time a dump-truck stop for us by Valsayn and we scramble up on the tray as the driver speed off. Is only then we realize that it was an empty sugar truck and the tray was pack up with red ants. Man, we get bite like crazy! And no matter how much we knocking on the glass and begging him to stop, he and the fraykoon-face loader killing they selves laughing in front. He carry us all the way down Princess Margaret Highway to Chaguanas before he stop the truck and let us off. You shoulda see us on the side of the highway stripping off all we clothes and beating off red ants from all over we skin while people in passing vehicles laughing and pointing at us like if we crazy.

One evening a fella down in Rio Claro come out from a rumshop and start up his land-rover, so Shah run up to him and ask if he could give us a ride. "Ah only goin' right up d'road," the fella say. "Is awright." Shah say, "We g'take you as far as yuh goin'." "Yeah, buh is only right up d'road." "Dat is okay" Shah say, and he call us, so we run and jump up on the land-rover. The fella start up and drive around the corner and pull into a yard; no more than two hundred yards. "Awright," he say "Ah reach home. Ah tell all you is right up d'road ah was goin'."

THIRTY

February 13th

I went to see Dr Timothy this morning. He told me again that I should spend a few days in the hospital so that they can monitor me properly, but again I refused.

After examining me, he prescribed some antibiotics for an ear infection he'd detected, and some different medications for the headaches and the cough.

I wish you were here to read my novel as it progresses. I'm shocked by the quality of my writing. At night I sit up in bed and read through my day's work and I'm amazed! I don't mean to sing my own praises, but I must express my satisfaction. I don't know how I do it. On mornings I pick up my pen and my whole being abandons me. My surroundings become obsolete and my mind runs amok. There's no real effort on my part anymore. The words flow as easily as I breathe.

I'm writing ceaselessly. At night before I sleep, I pray that I'll not lose the feel I've developed for my story. Each morning I wake up more excited and more eager to resume work on it. Every single thing I do is focused on its completion. It's all that matters to me now.

THIRTY ONE

Playful sunbeams
Sneaking through numerous creases
Tug gently at my heavy eyelids.
Morning scents of freshly cut grass,
Steaming, hand-grated cocoa
And saltfish frying in an iron pot
Excite my awakening nostrils.
Dogs barking, roosters crowing, horns beeping;
Market women chattering aloud
In sing-song voices;
A lone kiskedee serenading at my window;
Mother, busy, bustling about in the kitchen.
Time to wake up sleepy-head.
Brush your teeth and wash your face.
Change your clothes and comb your hair.
It's time for school!

THIRTY TWO

February 15th

I've surrendered myself to my art. There's no other way for me. Society holds nothing for me anymore. I have no other interests here, but this world which exists within my imagination.

All my life I've been striving to be a creative artist. I've written poetry since I was a child.

The passion was always in me but the ability to express my feelings had been difficult to develop.

I believe that we're all divided into two distinct groups, craftsmen and artists. The craftsman does. The artist feels. Society was built by and for the craftsman. He fits easily; but not the artist.

His gift is his burden. Few have been able to cope with it. Those who attained any success, did so only because they managed to master a craft as an outlet for their art.

Through constant diligence, they were able to harness their passion and, by manipulating some form of expression, to channel it into society's understanding and acceptance.

The craftsman is found pleasing because he satisfies our intellect.

But the artist?... Well, we both love and fear him, because he forces us to scrutinize ourselves, and that's a task with which we're never comfortable.

THIRTY THREE

I use to lie alone in mih bed for hours at night and think about things. In the next room Papa use to have we longtime Phillips radio tuned-in to the Windward Islands Broadcasting Service.

The music and the voices drifting across the ocean, and on rainy nights the raindrops beating a rhythm on we galvanize roof, and the frogs and toads croaking their love-songs in the pond outside, use to set mih mind on fire.

Late in the night, after the station sign off, and all you hearing from it is static, and Papa start snoring, and Mama get up to turn off the radio, and Mister Achang rumshop close up for the night, and the whole village was sleeping, I use to lie in bed and set mih imagination free.

The nights use to be so quiet then, except sometimes when there'd be an owl hooting near mih window, or a dog barking somewhere off in the distance, or the whistle of the wind in the coconut trees outside.

And always of course, old man Killer, boasting to the night about the glories of his stick-fighting days, as he drunkenly picked his way over the river, to his home in the barracks at Sticking Cherry Hill.

THIRTY FOUR

February 19th

I went to see Dr Timothy again this morning. I was really sick last night. I had a fever and a terrible headache and I vomited four times. He gave me two different kinds of medications and an injection, and set an appointment for me for next week Thursday.

I got so sick last night because yesterday I got soaked while taking a walk. I know that I was foolish not to shelter but it was a spring-like day and the rain was so inviting. From the time I got home out of the rain, I knew that I'd made a mistake.

I could feel the chill throughout my body. My nose was stuffed up and I was sneezing. I dried myself and changed into warm clothes, then drank some hot tea with lemon and honey, took two aspirins and climbed into bed. But I couldn't sleep. I was shivering even though I wrapped myself in a heavy blanket. I had roasting fever and an upset stomach, which kept me running to the bathroom to vomit.

For most of the night I lay awake in bed and thought of Joyce. I remembered the time we were speeding across the Utah Salt Flats in our old yellow Plymouth which she'd nicknamed "Kisskedee", with Janis Joplin screaming "Me and Bobby McGee" from the car radio; and my mouth was dry and salty; and she turned around, and kneeling on the front seat, she opened the styrofoam cooler in the back, and took out a container with chunks of honey-dew melon she'd cut up earlier in the day and put on ice; and she fed me as I drove; and the dryness and the saltiness disappeared.

And then I remembered us on Beale Street in Memphis, one April

Saturday night; with the sounds of Blues and Jazz and Rockabilly all around us; and it was raining; and we were soaking in each other's arms under a too small umbrella; and the rain water was seeping down my face onto my lips; and she was laughing.

Then we were at a powwow in the Black Hills, dancing and chanting with more than a hundred Lakota braves, at the base of the Crazy Horse memorial mountain; then racing along the rugged Big Sur coastline, on our way to join Cesar and his farm workers in Napa Valley; then shouting love messages to each other at Hell's Canyon on the Snake River in Idaho and listening for the echoes being flung back at us; then dodging alligators and armadillos in the Everglades as we cruised along the Alley from Ft Lauderdale to the Gulf coast; then gazing at the starlit sky from upon the open deck of a big wheeler on the mighty Mississippi.

I remembered us whale watching in Nantucket; and weathering a hurricane in the Keys; and herding cattle in the shadows of the Grand Tetons; and hiking Vermont's wildly colorful autumn trails; and sharing a hot apple dumpling smothered with vanilla ice cream at Knott's Berry Farm; and feasting on Jambalaya and crawfish to the sounds of Zydeco music on the Louisiana bayou; and shivering in the winter wonderland of Niagara at Christmastime.

And then I remembered how, after I'd stood in line for ten hours outside the Garden, for tickets to take her to see the King in concert, she'd buried her head in my chest and cried uncontrollably throughout the whole show.

I remembered us everywhere we used to be, and we were happy.

I finally fell asleep around 3.00am.

Underneath the heavy blanket, I sweated out my fever and I felt good when I woke up. Joyce always made me feel good. But my heart ached for her. So I sat on the bed and wrote her a love song. I used to write her many love songs. She used to like to hear me sing them to her in my raspy, unmelodious voice. They were mostly silly little verses but she used to love to hear them, especially when we were alone in the car on the road to nowhere in particular. And there were many such times.

THIRTY FIVE

If you return
These tears I shed will flow no more.
I'll love you much more than before.
I'll worship you from morn till night
And never let you from my sight.
Beside you I shall always be
If you return to me.

If you return,
Each rising of the morning sun
Will tell me that you are the one
Each whisper of the evening breeze
Will set my heavy heart at ease
Our lives will be a lasting spree
If you return to me.

If you return,
My darkness soon will disappear.
Your presence will soothe my every care.
No more at night time shall I dread
The quiet coldness of my bed.
Daylight once more shall I see
If you return to me.

If you return,
I shall for you do anything.
Tender love songs shall I sing.
I'll make for you a crown of gold
And never will my love grow old.
Never again shall I set you free
If you return to me.

THIRTY SIX

February 21st

I wish I could just pack up and come home right now. But first I must make every effort to finish my work. I cannot return unfulfilled. I have to complete this novel. I have to get it out of my system; to liberate myself; to cleanse myself of it.

I feel like I have to do this to be able to rediscover the innocence of my childhood when life was simple and light and full of wonder and mystery; when you and Mama and Papa and our village and our beloved country was my whole world; before this demon began to stalk me; before this obsession to divulge my thoughts and my feelings and my experiences began to possess me.

As soon as it's done and I submit it, I'll pack up and be on my way. Although I know that I'll miss Mama and Papa terribly and that life cannot be the same without them, still, home is home, and just the environment around the house will do much to soothe me.

It's strange isn't it that so many of us who leave home, are constantly in search of some way of returning.

I'm feeling very weak. I'm losing weight because I'm skipping too many meals. I just don't feel hungry. The new medications are very strong. They curb my appetite and make me feel light-headed.

THIRTY SEVEN

I remember your face, your loving embrace
Your twinkling eyes, your words always wise
The warmth of your breast, your gentle caress
Your silvery hair to which none can compare
Your voice soft and sweet, your radiance complete
The vision you granted, the dream you implanted
The needs often hidden, the praises forbidden
How you brushed off my tears and soothed my fears

Mother of peace
Never release
This heart which you hold.
None can replace
The stamp of your face
On my soul.
Others have come
And others have gone on before me;
Still do I see in your face,
The beginning and the end of my world.

THIRTY EIGHT

February 23rd

I'm afraid. The fever has returned, and since I woke up yesterday I've been having the shakes. I spent the whole day in bed, shivering under my blanket.

This morning I looked in the mirror and saw a stranger. I've lost so much weight. My eyes are sunken inside my head and I look twice my age. I haven't had a decent meal for over a week now. I've tried forcing myself to eat but everything leaves a bitter taste in my mouth. I can't stay on my feet for long without feeling faint.

I've hardly written anything for the past two days. I can't concentrate. Sometimes in the middle of a sentence I find my thoughts drifting off. I'm struggling to keep my mind focused, but it's becoming more and more difficult.

Now I've begun questioning my choices. Why am I subjecting myself to this? Why did I leave home in the first place? I didn't have to come here to write. I could've pursued my writing at home. Others have done it; and with much more success. Why did I think that it was so necessary for me to come here? I wish I could understand that.

Maybe I was fleeing from something or maybe I was trying to find something. Sometimes I try to rationalize it by thinking that because I grew up on a small island and was corralled by the sea on all sides, I felt a compulsion to expand my boundaries; a need to cross the waters. Now I long for the day when I can go home again.

THIRTY NINE

Like the ungrateful child,
Neglectful of the womb which gave him life;
Like the laden cherry branch
Which bows and bends, then breaks,
Burdened by the weight of its own productivity;
Like the single, solitary leaf, which falling,
Drifts aimlessly into some long meandering stream;
So is the one who turns his back
And yearns not for the land of his origin.

FORTY

February 24th

I've been having dizzy spells since yesterday and I still have the fever. All day today I've been in bed. I have aches all over and my body feels weak. When I get up to go to the bathroom, my head starts to pound and I feel giddy. I know it's because I haven't been eating properly. I just don't feel hungry.

Lately I've become aware of a growing discomfort in my joints. It's a kind of dull pain, which causes me to have to crack my joints for relief. But it's not really a pain. It's more like a stiffness; like if the bones in my joints get stuck together in their sockets and they need a little help to be prodded apart. I've been paying close attention to this phenomenon.

Each joint has its own individual motion to achieve the desired relief. For the shoulder it's a sudden upward jerk; the elbows, an outward arm fling; the wrist, an inner jerk; the fingers, a backward bend with the fingers of both hands intertwined; the ankles, a sudden outward instep stretch; the knees, a forward fling; the waist, a quick hip-thrust to each side; and the neck, a sudden head jerk to one side, then the other. Each motion produces a loud snapping sound that can be clearly heard and which brings instant relief.

It's weird. I might've been experiencing this for a while and never noticed. It's probably some sort of arthritis setting in.

FORTY ONE

In the evening's ghostly shadows
When the winter ocean rages,
And multitudes of workers
Hurry homeward to their cages.
At twilight's fading brightness
When all birds seek one direction,
And the wind blows cold and fiercely,
Fiercely from across the ocean.
In the evening when my lover
Whispers words of love and laughter,
I turn inward to myself,
I turn inward to myself.

At night when all is silent
And the world is still and black;
When in waves my life reminds me
Of the happiness I lack.
When night-sounds like the chiming
Of a chapel's funeral bells
Whisper thoughts of long lost childhood;
Whisper while the aching swells.
When a distant dog's cry warns me
Of the cold grave up ahead,
I turn inward to myself,
I turn inward to myself.

FORTY TWO

February 25th

You'll never guess who I saw today. I was feeling really nauseous from the medications so I opened the window for some air. I glanced down and there was Teacher Toney. Remember I told you I thought I'd seen him one day in Times Square. Now I'm sure it was he.

When I saw him today he was standing at the bus stop across the street from my room. Before I could react the bus pulled up and he disappeared inside.

I didn't know that he was up here. Is he living here now? He was wearing some kind of uniform so he must be working somewhere.

Now I'd never discussed this with anyone before, not even you. But all during my growing up years back home there'd been a strange and hostile relationship between him and me. It was a resentment which was relayed only by eye contact and never faded with the passage of time. This goes back to when I was in Exhibition class and he was still teaching at our school.

The strange thing is, he was my favorite teacher for a while because he'd taken a special interest in my poems. He'd critique them and encourage me to continue writing. He'd said that there was a certain buoyancy in my verse and he was convinced that I could do well if I kept at it. He was the one who turned me on to the music and rhythms of poetry.

He'd loved to recite the verses of the old English masters, Shelley, Keats, Shakespeare, Burns, Arnold and Tennyson. But the ones he seemed to cherish most were the poems of William Wordsworth. To hear him recite 'The Solitary Reaper' or 'The Daffodils' or 'Lines written above Tintern

Abbey' was like hearing a chorus of semps, picoplats, and bullfinches or the babbling waters of the Caura and the Aripo rivers, rolling and tumbling over boulders, rocks and pebbles.

It was as if he tasted the words. Like they were delicious to him, swirling and twirling in his mouth, caressing his tongue and his lips as they flowed out. He loved the rhythms of poetry and I grew to love those same rhythms because of him. He was my mentor and I idolized him.

Those were the days when his son Samuel was my best friend. Sam and I were inseparable. We did everything together. Then one day it all changed.

You remember Coronation Day when all the schools from the area had gathered in the savannah for a rally and everyone was dressed in starched and ironed uniforms and carefully folded socks and blancoed crepesoles? And while waiting for the Inspector of Schools to arrive for the ceremony, and we were all becoming bored and restless, and the teachers had everyone practicing 'God save the Queen' and 'Rule Britannia', some of the boys had sneaked off and gone to swim in the river? And Pips from down by the standpipe, in his usual daredevil style, and dressed in his full school uniform, started climbing up a fat bamboo that leaned over the water? And when he got to where he was about thirty feet high, he stood up, lifted his hands over his head and shouted 'Meee Tarzannnn!!'? And striking a Tarzan pose he began the Tarzan yell? 'AhWohhh Ohhhhhhhh!!' And how just then, with a loud crack, the bamboo broke and he fell screaming, 'Oh God...Help! Help!' into the muddy river? And luckily Parrot was cutting grass for his cattle down there at the same time, he had to jump in and pull him out? And how pandemonium broke out among the thousands of students when, wet and muddied he ran across the crowded savannah, zig-zagging through the schools' formations, with about fifty of us boys following behind, all yelling like Tarzan, while the teachers ran around screaming and trying to restore order?

Well when we got to the road we ran smack into Teacher Toney, my favorite teacher, my mentor, poetry lover, sensitive champion of the rhythm of verse. But he was none of those things on that day. That day he was a different person. That day he was like a madman! He was fuming! His eyes were bulging and red and his body shook with rage, because he was the chief organizer of that rally and we had dared to disrupt it.

Screaming 'Animals!! Stop it!! Stop it at once!!!' at the top of his voice, he waded into the crowd, grabbed Samuel and me out of the whole procession, pulled off his belt and began flailing away at us like a madman, screaming at us that we were behaving like hooligans; then focusing his fury on me, he accused me of encouraging Samuel in this hooliganism and of intentionally disrupting his efforts.

That day in his anger he berated me, saying that I was a bad influence on his son; that I'd better keep away from him; and that I'd never amount to anything. He said that I was a nobody now, and that I'd always be a nobody.

I couldn't believe what was happening. I couldn't believe the hate spewing from his mouth; the same mouth which just yesterday was brimming with praise for my poem "The Three Sisters of the Southern Range".

His words stung like Congo pepper. I locked my eyes to his in disbelief and defiance but I couldn't control the tears welling up in them and beginning to roll down my cheeks.

Through a teary haze I could see the shocked faces of friends and neighbors who were gathered around; Cinty from the shop, Bowery the nuts man, Sakeena the bara lady, Pingo the pace bowler from Pleasant Hill, Allan from Standard Six and Rajah from the scout troop. They were all staring in shock. They'd all witnessed my denigration by him. He'd placed a deep dent on my ego.

Strangely though, his attitude that day seemed to have had a much more devastating effect on Samuel whose life would eventually spin out of control.

Although our families remained friendly over the years, Teacher Toney and I had always viewed each other from a distance after that, never exchanging a word with each other again.

FORTY THREE

"Twelve O' Clock every night Mr. Semper grave does open up, and he does get out and siddong on top of his tombstone."
"Who tell you dat?!"
"PeeWee. He see him plenty times."
"Dat eh true."
"Is true! Before he dead, he use t'deal with d'devil. D'night after dey bury him, he come back as a big white horse. Plenty people see it runnin' all arong d'village."
"Ha! Ha! Ha! Dat wasn't Mr Semper. Dat horse is d'Pahyol man one from Enterprise. Dat PeeWee only puttin' ah set ah schupidness in yuh head, yes."
"Is d'truth man. PeeWee have a special gift. He does see things."
"Boy, you eh play you dotish nah! Why you does believe everything dat drunkard PeeWee tellin' you? He crazy yes. Ent he say dat he d'see a merrymaid one night dong by d'creek when he was comin' back home from a wake in Fyzabad, and how she was callin' him out in d'sea, and how he park-up his bike by d'sea-wall next to Godineau bridge, and strip off all his clothes, and jump in d'water, and swim behind she all d'way out to Faralon; and how dey spend d'rest ah d'night out dere drinkin' pommerack wine and makin' love and thing? And a next time, ent he say how he d'see a spaceship, about d'size ah Sahaboo jitney, land by d'river, and how when he gone dong dere, he see a set ah lil two-head and three-head space people drinkin' puncheon and fetein' in d'bamboo patch? And dey arks him to join d'party and he teach dem how to wine and den he break a piece ah cassava stick and show dem how to limbo? And he say how most ah dem coulda limbo lower

dan d'dancers in Arawak dance troupe? You eh see d'man wheel missin' a few spokes!? Ha! Ha! Ha!"

"Yeah, you laugh man. You must be jealous dat you cyar see d'things he does be seein'."

"Boy, you's a real bobolee yes."

"I bet you a dollar you cyar go in d'cemetary twelve o'clock tonight and siddong on Mr. Semper grave."

"What?!"

"I bet you cyar go in d'cemetary midnight tonight and siddong on Mr. Semper grave."

"Why?"

"If PeeWee lyin' den you eh go fraid."

"Cheups!..You crazy yes; you know dat? You gett'n crazy just like he."

"Well bet mih nah!"

"Cheups!! Me eh have time with you nah. You crazy just like he."

FORTY FOUR

February 26th

I could barely stand up this morning, I was so weak. I called Dr Timothy, and he must've detected the panic in my voice, because he told me to come to his office right away. I had to ask Mrs Kaminsky my landlady, to get a taxi to take me there.

When the doctor saw me, he immediately made arrangements to have me warded at Bellevue. At first I tried to resist, but he refused to listen. He was really angry, even shouting at me because I'd missed my appointment on Thursday.

He accused me of being careless and of deliberately sabotaging my own health. He said that in my present condition, he wasn't giving me a choice anymore; that since I wasn't making any effort to take care of myself, he was going to place me where others can take care of me.

I tried telling him that I had to be at home because I was working on my novel and that it was nearing completion. He told me that whatever I wanted to do will have to be done at the hospital.

FORTY FIVE

Throbbing jukebox songs
Seeping through my keyhole,
Somehow bring to mind a time,
Not too long past,
When mother, wrinkled and gray,
Kissed my cheeks
And soothed my fears away.

FORTY SIX

February 27th

By the time they admitted me yesterday I was really sick. My fever was so intense that I was becoming delirious. I can recall the ambulance arriving for me at Dr Timothy's office, but not much more.

I remember my head was pounding with an incessant rhythm as distorted images of characters, whose antics used to frighten me as a child, raced through my mind in rapid succession; grinning faces, each rushing madly towards me, then receding in a yoyo-like motion, while another rushed in to take its place.

There was Mahal the busless bus driver, and Crazy Baby who was always fixing her hair; and Oblijay who would pelt bottles and stones for no reason, and Pro with his bag of bones of children he'd eaten; and Kyaho and Saga and Kenny, and Saroop and Bharp and ShadowBenny; and MookMook and Pelly and Cocksin, and Bennah and SwellyBelly and Gwendolyn; and Brigo and Guana and Surujbal, and Plocks who used to play gorilla for carnival; and....and....

Everything was kind of blurry after that. The last thing I recall was getting a painful injection on my hip but I'm not sure where I was at the time. After that, as I drifted in and out of consciousness, I could vaguely recall being placed in a bed and being hooked up to all kinds of tubes and gadgets.

FORTY SEVEN

*Plagued by thoughts of my insignificance,
I sat among discarded copra shells
Littering the barren seashore;
Envying the squirrels playing amongst the palms
And the dancing waves kissing the sand.
Then she passed by
And looked at me and smiled and took my hand.
Like a child I followed,
Crying my sorrows upon her shoulder;
But she just laughed
And sang her song of love's sweet pleasures.
Her beauty and her radiance enlightened my path
As she led me on.*

FORTY EIGHT

March 1st

Oh God! Oh God! What're they doing to me!!? The pain is too much!! I can't stand it. They've implanted a needle somewhere in my waist and it's killing me. Millions of tiny creatures are crawling all through my body! All over my head, in my eyes, my ears, my nose, my throat, my tongue, my lips; all down my back, in my legs, up my arms, down to my toes and my fingertips! I'm burning up! There's a heat inside me! I'm on fire! My muscles feel limp. My bones ache. My throat is parched. I feel like vomiting all the time. I want to get up; to rip away all this apparatus from me; to stretch my limbs; to bend my back; to crack my joints. But I can't move. My body refuses to respond. When I fart it feels like a fireball inside me. I want to pee all the time but it burns like pepper. I'm constipated and my belly is bloated. Doc, why don't you help me!? Nurse, give me something! Give me anything to make me sleep; to make me die; to take me away from this hell!!

FORTY NINE

"Mama?"
"Sonny?"
"I cyah sleep."
"Come lie dong over here by me."
"I only tossin' and turnin' in mih bed."
"Me too."
"You worryin' about me?"
"I cyah help it son."
"I g'be awright."
"So you really goin' tomorrow."
"I have t'go Ma."
"You must write we often."
"Every week Ma. I promise"
"Make sure and eat good, and wear warm clothes."
"Yes."
"And if you get sick, doh hide it from we."
"No mama."
"And ley we know about any problems you havin'.
"Yes mama."
"You's a good son."
"Ma?"
"Yes?"
"Is awright if I sleep here tonight?"
"Yes."
"Tomorrow night I go be so far away."
"I know, son. I know."

FIFTY

March 3rd

I'm not eating or drinking anything here at the hospital. They're giving me all my nutrients and a whole slew of medications intravenously. I must be getting some very strong medicine because I'm drugged-up all the time now. But my fever and headache still haven't gone away.

Remember I'd mentioned that when I saw Teacher Toney, waiting that day for the bus, he was wearing a uniform? Well guess what. He's working right here at the hospital. I caught a glimpse of him out of the corner of my eye today. He was passing by my room, pushing an empty wheelchair. He glanced my way as he passed. He didn't approach me though. I'm not sure he recognized me.

FIFTY ONE

Is a long time since I use to be able to dash across a football field, dribbling the ball in front of me as I rush towards the opposite goal, dodging in and out and around them fellas like a real pro.

Is a long time since I use to hear mih friends and them bawling and clapping and calling-out mih name as I make a grand-charge to kick the ball in one corner of the goal, and as the goalie dive, I sneak it inside the next corner, leaving him like a real imps, to absorb all kinds of fatigue and picong from the crowd.

I was an awright player in them days, yes. I use to kick good with mih two feet, and I was real fast on the field. I was so good, I coulda even make mih high school team for Intercol, but I didn't show up for the trials. I didn't have no football togs. Mih parents couldn't afford it. They use to have it up to here just paying mih school fees and mih passage, and buying books and uniform for me.

FIFTY TWO

March 4th

Teacher Toney came into my room last night. It was late; well past midnight. The whole ward was quiet. Everyone was asleep, except me. I was lying in bed, hooked up to all kinds of monitors and contraptions, with my eyes closed, remembering our cattle and how we would tie them out in the pasture every morning before going to school.

There was Mamazie and Papazie and the two heifers we named Cherry Pink and Apple Blossom.

I was remembering how at midday, when we went home for lunch, we'd carry two buckets full of mahrr for them, or a mixture of water and molasses, or water with a little flour and salt for taste; and how they'd start mooing from the time they saw us coming; and how in the evening, just before it got dark, we'd untie their ropes and race behind them as they galloped home to their pen behind the house.

I was thinking about how we'd run late sometimes because we'd stop to pick dongs from the tree behind the watchman's hut or we'd been playing windball cricket in the park with Ulric and them. And how they'd moo and moo and create such a ruckus when they saw us coming, as if complaining to the whole neighborhood because we were a little late.

I was thinking of how excited we were when Mama and Papa first brought home Mamazie and Papazie. They'd bought them from Hassanali Nana in Piparo and walked all the way from there with them. He'd told them that it was real hard for him to sell his two favorite animals but he was too old now and would be unable to continue taking proper care of them, especially as Mamazie was expecting to put down anytime soon. She was so full, they said they had to walk slowly and stop to rest many times along the way.

When she gave birth about a week later, she had two calves which was cause for much celebration at home. Mama and Papa said that they were ours and we named them Cherry Pink and Apple Blossom after the popular English song.

I had settled deep within that world of my childhood memories, when I was suddenly snapped out of it by what sounded like a hushed giggle. It took a great effort to open my eyes, the lids felt so heavy. But when I did, there he was, Teacher Toney, sitting in the dim light at the table in the corner with his empty wheelchair parked next to him.

I looked closely and noticed that he was reading. I squinted and peered closer and realized that it was one of my notebooks with my unfinished novel he was reading.

How did he get his hands on that?! Mrs Kaminsky brought them here just this morning. She didn't want to leave them on the table where anyone could just walk in, pick them up and start reading so she made the nurse place them inside the drawer in the stand beside my bed.

What gave him the right to enter my room uninvited, go through my personal belongings, and invade the privacy of my story?! Especially him, who'd wounded my ego on that long ago Coronation Day by denigrating me in the presence of so many people.

I felt a rage building inside me. I wanted to jump off the bed and confront him but I couldn't move. I tried shouting but no sound came out.

He was giggling as he read. What was he giggling about?! My novel is not a comedy! That's a serious story, Teach! I've poured my heart and soul into those pages! What's so funny?!

He giggled and snickered and struggled to stifle a hushed laugh.

I was furious! I wanted to scream at him; to fly off my bed; to seize him by the throat; to pulverize him; to mash him up like a bug; but I couldn't move. I just lay there, motionless.

"Too much self-indulgence!" he hissed under his breath, "Not enough focus! The story is all over the place. There must be focus like the point of a needle; and real emotion. It must come from the heart!"

Then his mood changed and he was angry. Like on that Coronation Day, his eyes were bulging in his head as he scrambled to his feet, glaring scornfully at me.

"Where's the beauty?!.... Where's the joy...the innocence?!.... Where's the rhythm?!...." he growled, "What happened to my poet from our Exhibition Class?!!!"

Then he dropped my notebook on the floor, grabbed his wheelchair, turned around and stormed out of the room.

FIFTY THREE

Love them,
Though they strew your path with thorns
And set their dogs upon you.

Bless them,
Though they pay no heed
Or say your words are words of folly.

Forgive them,
Though they fill your name with slander
As they drive you to your grave.

They say you are a fool
For loving things of no importance;
But they are lost,
And being lost,
They are afraid of you.

FIFTY FOUR

March 7th

I'm confused! How can you say that Teacher Toney had drowned in Balandra last July, when I see him here? I'm sure it's he. I see him every day.

You said in your letter that Tanty Rita went on the Friendly Society's excursion when he'd disappeared. But if he'd drowned, then who've I been seeing here? Who did I see at the bus stop? Who did I see pushing an empty wheelchair in the hospital corridor? Who came into my room the other night, read my material, then laughed and belittled me? Was it all a dream?! Is he a figment of my imagination that's just trying to torment me?! Trying to hurt me?! Trying to seek revenge for something?!...Is this all about that incident in the park on Coronation Day? Or is it about what happened to his son Samuel?!...Could that have something to do with this?!

It wasn't my fault that Samuel turned out the way he did. He wasn't my friend when he'd dropped out of Benedicts and started drinking and gambling and hanging out and getting into trouble with the law. He wasn't with me when he freaked out and left home and went to live with the jamette lady by the trainline, and then when she threw him out he went off and became a vagrant in Port of Spain and would have nothing to do with anybody. In those days, before that happened to him, he was liming with his badjohn friends from the gambling club behind Union Park. That's how he ended-up like that.

I had nothing to do with it! We'd gone our separate ways long before that; ever since we started college. He went to St. Benedicts, I to Presentation. We developed different circles of friends. We hardly ever saw each other. It wasn't my fault! Teacher Toney knows it and I know it. He's the one who'd forced the split! I won't accept the blame!

Just because we were part of a boyhood prank on Coronation Day so many years ago, does it mean that I must continue to carry blame for every stupid, reckless incident in his life afterwards!? I refuse to bear the weight of that albatross around my neck!!

I'm going to have to confront Teacher Toney and clear the air. There's no reason for this to continue. We're too far from home to be waging this mental warfare; too far removed from those early school days to be carrying a grudge for an incident that should no longer be of any significance to either of us.

FIFTY FIVE

There was a time when I could sing
When I could sing of anything
Of thieves and clowns and queens and kings
There was a time
There was a time.

There was a time when I could dance
When I could dance like in a trance
From waltz to wine, pliay to prance
There was a time
Oh what a time

There was a time when I could smile
When I could smile like one beguiled
By pleasures or by passions wild
There was a time
A lovely time

There was a time when I could dream
When I could dream of any theme
Make sorrows no more what they seem
There was a time
Another time.

FIFTY SIX

March 8th

I'm feeling a little better this morning so Dr. Timothy brought Dr. Woo, a specialist, to explain their diagnosis to me. He says that there's an imbalance in the ratio of red and white cells in my blood, and this could be the cause of all my ailments. Some mutant cells have developed and may be affecting my immune system, making it difficult for my body to fight off infections.

Last week, when I was admitted to the hospital, they'd given me the first round of a course of medications aimed at destroying these mutant cells. They are very strong drugs with serious physical and mental side effects. They caused me more pain than I'd ever known before.

The problem however, is that along with the mutant cells, some of my normal cells are also being destroyed. This, they claim, is an unavoidable result of the process.

Today I've been able to sit up in bed so I made a few halting attempts to continue writing. The nurses allowed me to use a breakfast cart, which slides right over my bed, making a convenient desk, but it was no use. I sat there for most of the day with pen in hand, but nothing was forthcoming. Although I've come a long way with my novel this time, I'm afraid that once again, I may not be able to complete it.

FIFTY SEVEN

There is just one thing that I dread
With indescribable horror,
And that is that one day
When I'm old and grey
And my back is bent,
When my limbs are aching
And my strength is spent,
I might look back on my life and discover
That in my youth
I was too afraid
To pursue my heart's desire.

FIFTY EIGHT

March 9th

I received your letter today and when I read it, I broke down and wept. To be home again among familiar faces, with the tropic sun to greet me on mornings and the wind in the bamboo patch at night to soothe my mind, is more than I can hope for.

My dear, dear sister, what have I ever done to deserve you? Your offer overwhelms me but now it's out of my hands. The hospital won't release me. My doctors won't allow it. Besides, all my care is being covered by my health insurance from the job. I can't afford it otherwise. I'm a prisoner here. They monitor me constantly.

I lie here and reflect on my lifestyle and the path I'd taken and I don't know what to make of it. Maybe I'd lost myself in some kind of fantasy. Maybe I'd been struggling to fit a mould, which wasn't made for me.

I can recall that even in those early days at home, when life was all joy and fun and laughter, this demon had already begun to possess me.

In the privacy of my mind, I'd fought against it with all of my might. But I could never completely exorcise it.

During the entire length of my adult life, while I'd lived and studied and worked and progressed, I was never free of it.

And during my years with Joyce all I ever wrote were my love songs to her. I never felt the need to write anything else because I was happy just being in her company. With her I was able to rediscover the serenity, the security and the simple pleasures I'd known in my childhood with you and Mama and Papa.

But then, when I lost her, that same demon from my youth began its assault again. I needed to shield myself so I turned to my pen for comfort. I started to write again.

I wish now that I had done more for her. I should've recognized at the time how serious her illness was. I should never have allowed her to go back to her family. They must've felt vindicated to have her back. No wonder they made sure I never saw her again.

FIFTY NINE

Just now I doze off and dream about cascadoo, curry cascadoo. Not no big and huksy Guyanese hassah or no plain old flat-head chahtow. I dream about the real thing; young and sweet and juicy; round-head, mud-loving Trini cascadoo; curry down dry with sadah roti, or with plain white-rice and dhal, or with boil-down ground provisions.

And not no so-called, make-believe curry cascadoo either, swimming in long, long curry water, with a set of quarter-moon-shaped scales floating all over the plate like some grayish-black, mucksy big-toe nails. Mm...mm; I talking about curry cascadoo like what mih Tantee Dooye use to make. Curry cascadoo so delicious, just the thought of it use to make yuh mouth water and use to make you bite yuh tongue everytime you taste it. I tell you, nobody couldn't touch Tantee Dooye when it come to cooking curry cascadoo.

I remember how she use to take the fish and cut open the belly, and clean out the inside, and dig out the gills and the eyes, and trim off the tail and the fins and the whiskers. Then she use to wash them out a few times with some fresh rough-back lemon, and scrub out the scales from every fish, one by one, with an old toothbrush she had just for that, then rinse them clean and dry them off. Then she use to grind up plenty podina, and bandania and chive and fine-thyme and bud-pepper and onion and garlic on she stone seal. Then she use to mix that up with enough of she own curry mixture she use to make by grinding up massala seeds and mayhtee and jeerah and anchar massala and some dry harrdee root. Then she use to add some crush-up tomatoes and salt and sour tambran to make a paste. Then she use to stuff all the fish with about half of the paste, making sure she full up the belly and the head area. Then she use to cut up a few more small tomatoes, some more chive and onions, and throw them in a basin with the fish and the rest of the paste, and well mix up all that together.

Then she use to cover the basin and let it sit for about an hour. Then when she ready, she use to heat up some oil in she old iron pot till it hot, hot. Then when it start to bubble-up and smoke, she use to empty-out everything from the basin inside the pot and let it chong-kay good for a few minutes, turning it all the time. Then she use to cover the pot, reduce the heat and let it cook down dry only turning it a few times for it to cook evenly. Everybody use to talk about Tanty Dooye curry cascadoo. Nobody couldn't step in she shoes when it come to cooking curry cascadoo.

I was dreaming about how Easter weekend use to always be cascadoo holiday time for us; how we use to go by Sundar Khaka in Biche for the whole weekend. He use to live alone and plant garden and sell in the market. His house was a big carat house near the road, but he had about forty acres in the back with cocoa and orange and coconut and fig and yam and cassava and all kinds of vegetables and fruits. Almost anything you could think about, Sundar Khaka had. Plus he use to mind ducks and fowls and cattle and goats; and because his land d'boundary the government forest, it use to have endless wild beast. You coulda always get some kind of wild meat by him.

I was dreaming about how Mama and Papa use to load us up in the car after Jummah prayers every Good Friday and we use to stop and pick up Choonksie Bhowjee and she daughters Sabeeta and Sumintra in Sanko Road on we way down to Biche. Boboy Chacha and Zeena Chachee and their three children Abbie, Moomie and Taj use to come in their car and Tanty Dooye and Uncle Breds with their two sons Raj and Rohan and three daughters Seema, Shanti and Meena in their own. And Sundar Khaka use to always tell a few of his friends and their children from the village.

When we reach there, it use to be almost dusk-dark already. We use to start playing with we cousins and we friends from the village and the big people use to knock down a few drinks before the men start playing all-fours and the ladies start to cook. We food that night use to always be kitchree with cuchela, mango chutney and tum-tum because Good Friday was strictly a no-meat day.

I was dreaming about how we use to have to get up next morning before sun come up, because Saturday was we 'Cascadoo Catching Day'. We use to eat we belly full of sadah roti with bygan chokah or fry aloo and drown it down with a cup of hot cocoa tea, then all man had to head down by the river, way down in the cocoa field behind the house to a special area near a big savonet tree.

Over there the river had a deep curve and it form a pool. But the edge of the water was shallow and had plenty soharie-leaf plants growing in the swampy mud and the cascadoo did like to spawn there.

The first thing we had to do was to build a dam. It was plenty work so everybody had to pitch in and help.

Uncle Breds and Boboy Chacha had to dig dirt from the riverbank and the rest of us had to throw for Sundar Khaka and Papa in the water to build the dam. They had to build two mud banks about thirty feet apart to block off any water flowing in or out of the savonet-area pool. Then all of us use to start bailing out the water from the pool.

The work was hard and use to take up the whole day, but when you see we bail out most of the water and get down to mud, we just had to pick up cascadoo. All around we feet, all over the place, cascadoo jumping up like peas! Every Easter is about two to three pitch-oil tin of cascadoo we catching! And we use to also catch about a bucket full of other kinds of fish and small shrimps and crabs too. When we done, we just had to break the bank and flood up the river again.

Afterwards when we tote everything back by the house, we had to help wash and clean all the fish. By the time we done, it use to be dark already. The ladies use to season-up and fry-dry all the wahbeen and mamataytah and coscorob and small shrimps and crabs that we catch, and that with rice and dhal and a pepper salad was we Glorious Saturday dinner. Then everybody use to hit the sack.

I was dreaming about Easter Sunday. That was we real curry cascadoo feast day. The big people use to get up first and do all the work and let the children sleep late because of how much work we d'do the day before.

The men use to go with Sundar Khaka in the land to dig ground-provisions and cut fig and pick coconuts and breadfruits, and the ladies use to start cooking. As usual Tanty Dooye was in charge of the cascadoo seasoning and cooking and while the cooking going on the neighbors who come to help with the preparations, use to leave and go home to change and come back.

Time we wake up about twelve o'clock, all the food use to be ready already and laid out on the long table Sundar Khaka use to borrow every year from the mandir.

It use to have boil and fry yam, mataburro fig, tum-tum and cassava; rice, dhal, lentils, dhal-puree and parata; pigeon-peas with tannia, shatine, pumpkin, boil dasheen and eddoes; roast breadfruit, fry moko, slice-up cucumber and tomatoes; krestles, lettuce, mango anchar and karr-hee; chaltah, channa and aloo, khalounjee and pomseetay tal-karie.

But the main dish, everyman's wish; the cream of the crop, the star at the top; the jewel in the crown, the salt of the ground; the rainbow's end, the belly best friend, was always Tanty Dooye curry cascadoo! Cook down dry with only a hint of sulwah. A whole wedding-pot full! Covered with sooharie leaves and sitting proudly on a brick choolha.

By half past one all the work use to be finish, and everybody use to done bathe and dress up nice, and the neighbors use to start arriving.

I was dreaming about how the first thing everybody use to do was head straight for the food-table. Nobody ent serving nobody. You just take out how much you want and eat.

After first belly-full, we use to all go outside in the front yard for we every year Easter Sunday underhand, windball-cricket match. Papa and Uncle Breds use to always be captains and they use to pick the teams making sure that everybody get a game. We use to have so much fun, with plenty noise and clapping and laughing! And we use to always have two pails of coconut ice-cream for the game, that the neighbours use to bring.

After the game over, and the place start to turn dusk-dark, we use to go back inside and eat again. Then the big people would tackle the Oak and the Vat, and the music would start. Sundar Khaka would bring out his harmonium, Papa his dholak, Boboy Chacha his dhantal and Uncle Breds his mouth-organ.

Talk about fete! They use to play and sing whole night. And the ladies too use to sing and clap and dance and beat lotah and tarriah with big pennies; and you could hear them shouting and laughing hard hard. We and all use to leave we games sometimes and join in the merriment; singing and clapping and chamkaying with them. When day clean and the Vat and the Oak bottles empty, is only then they use to break up the lime and go to sleep.

I was dreaming about how when we get up Easter Monday in the afternoon-time, still tired, and the big people stale-booze from the night before, and hungry killing we skin, it use to have enough leftover food from we curry cascadoo feast yesterday to eat we belly full again, and to pack a parcel for everybody to carry home with them.

I was dreaming about waving goodbye to everybody as we start driving away in the evening; about Sundar Khaka and his friends from Biche, and Boboy Chacha and Zeena Chachee and mih cousins Abbie, Moomie and Taj, and Choonksie Bhowjee and she daughters Sabeeta and Sumintra who we use to drop-off back in Sanko Road on we way home, and Mama and Papa and you and me, and Uncle Breds and Tanty Dooye with their two sons Raj and Rohan and three daughters Seema, Shanti and Meena.

I was dreaming about Easter weekend and the pool by the savonet tree, and the cricket match, and bailing the river, and the music and the games and the ice-cream and the booze for the big people and all the food, especially the cascadoo.

Yes, I was dreaming about cascadoo...cascadoo...cascadoo...Just now I doze off and dream about cascadoo...curry cascadoo...Tanty Dooye's curry cascadoo.

SIXTY

March 10th

God, how I miss Joyce! She was still so young! Still so full of life! You'd have really liked her! I wish we had known each other back home before we came up here. We used to enjoy spending hours at a time recalling places and times when our paths might've crossed.

She was from Arouca and said that she visited the Scout's Jamboree at Valsayn everyday for the two weeks it was there. Our troop was there for the whole time, yet we'd never met.

Our paths might've crossed at Jayland Fair or for Dimache Gras in the Savannah when Sparrow sang "Dan is the Man" or for Siparee Mai celebrations, which our families never missed.

Her grandparents on her mother's side are from upper Caratal, near Kanchan Hill, so she'd spent many school holidays there. But we'd never met. Although she said that she remembered seeing "Loving You" at our cinema when it first showed there. And like us, she was at the Sunday matinee show. She too was a big Elvis fan. We'd driven to Memphis twice to visit Graceland and to Tupelo once to see the cottage where he'd lived as a child.

I heard that her ashes were sent to her grandparents in Caratal and they had it buried in a cemetery up there. She used to talk about them a lot. She used to always write to them about me. She used to promise me that we'd visit them one day.

SIXTY ONE

Remember me, my dear
When I have gone away;
When blossoms bow their heads in prayer
And raging mountain streams convey
Heart-broken Nature's tears.

Remember me
When monstrous hurricanes protest my death;
When oceans sob
And children cease their play.

Remember me
When black clouds burst
And angry lightening streaks
Attack the earth;
When forest trees fall to the ground and weep;
And death of life
Precedes its birth;

Remember me
When sorrow hastens to embrace
And loving thoughts refuse to stay;
When gentle lambs grow fierce
And savage beasts slink fearfully away,
Remember all we'd seen and done together.

And when at dismal night-time
Faintly pattering raindrops
Beat their funeral chants
Upon your galvanized cottage roof,
Remember me
And how much more we'd planned to do
If only I had lived.

Then if your soul should grieve,
Be not afraid to tear your hair
And pour your heart asunder
And wring your hands
And beat your breast
And weep and wail;
Not just for me,
But for the passing
Of a love that used to be.

SIXTY TWO

March 11th

These days I think constantly of home. Flashes of a happier time, when we were young and innocent and I was still free from the burdens of ambition, present themselves in rapid succession.

How many times upon Mayaro's golden sands, we'd greeted the first approaches of the dawn as the ocean wind dusted our sleep-worn eyes and the rolling waves danced around our feet.

How many days of roaming the mountains and valleys of the three ranges, we'd felt the throbbing soul of our beloved country.

How many Ramadan sunsets we'd hurried from home in answer to the muezzin's call from the mosque.

How many nights beneath the starlit sky we'd sat, cushioned in the company of friends, conversing on every conceivable subject.

Days and nights; weeks, months and years of constant growth, where are they all now?

Desperately I struggle to revive even a glimmer of those former times.

Desperately I grope within the deepest chambers of my mind, hoping to retrieve some remnant of that long lost era.

SIXTY THREE

"Sis! Look at dis!!"
"Jeez!! Boy, he pretty eh!? Where you get him?"
"Me and Hollis just ketch him in d'pasture"
"Hear how he whistlin' boy!"
"You like him?"
"Yeah, I like him!"
"Well, he's yours."
"Mine?!...Y..You...serious?!!"
"He's yours."
"Oh God. He so pretty! I g'call him Nightingale."
"Nightingale?!"
"Yes. Nightingale. A pretty name for a pretty bird."
"But he's a pico."
"So?"
"You cyar call a pico Nightingale."
"Why not?"
"Cause it doh sound right."
"How you mean it doh sound right?"
"Cause is two different things. A pico is a pico and a nightingale is a nightingale. And besides dat, you never see no nightingale in yuh life. We eh have none in Trinidad; not even in d'zoo."
"Ent you say he's mine?"
"Yes."
"Den I could call him anything I want."
"I know. But ...."

"I say he name Nightingale!.....Nightingale, Nightingale, Nightingale!"
"Okay! Okay! But is d'schupidest thing I ever hear in mih life. A pico name Nightingale…. Ssscccheupssss!"

SIXTY FOUR

March 12th

I'm coming home! Teacher Toney said that he will arrange it. Ever since I confronted him about the tensions between us, he's been so apologetic and so helpful to me. When I asked him about the Balandra incident that you'd mentioned, his only response was that that was a day of transformation for him.

He claimed that he'd stopped living the day Samuel had left home. He said that his heart had been broken twice; first when his wife had died and then when he'd lost Samuel. Afterwards his life had become a lie. He'd presented a brave front to everyone but the pain in his heart had kept growing in intensity. Finally he'd decided to escape it all by turning a new leaf and trying to live out the rest of his life as if those years had never happened.

He says that now, since our paths have crossed again, he's feeling a sense of camaraderie that he'd thought was lost forever. Now he wants only to make amends for the wrongs he may have done to all the people in his past who had believed in him, beginning with me.

For the past two days he's been spending most of his time sitting by my bedside, squeezing my head, massaging my shoulders, and talking about the good old days. He talks about the days when Samuel and I were close friends. He says that he remembers how happy Samuel was in those days. Since meeting me again he thinks more and more about Samuel and hopes that somehow this will lead to a reconciliation with his son.

He seems like his old self again, reciting his favorite Wordsworth poems to me with the joy and exuberance of the days when I was a student in Exhibition class and he was the School Leaving teacher at our school. He's my only friend here now. He's my mentor and my guide, and he makes me feel special again.

The doctors have scheduled another round of heavy medications for me for the 22nd of this month. They say it's to flush out the remaining bad cells from my body. But I don't want it. My body can't take it. They must know how hard it is. My God! What are they trying to do to me!? I haven't recovered from the last one yet and they're ready to put me through that hell again!

They claim that it must be done; that my body must be cleansed of the diseased cells before they can do anything more. But still they offer no guarantees that I'll be cured.

Well, I've made up my mind. I have to get away from here. I must escape their clutches. I've become just an experiment to them. Teach agrees. He believes that some time at home will rejuvenate me. I told him that Dr. Timothy and Dr. Woo won't allow it. He said that I shouldn't worry; that he'll take care of everything. He said that he was willing to do anything to make up for all the years he'd blamed me wrongfully for Samuel.

SIXTY FIVE

Go swiftly into blackness
When your sun descends,
Betraying not your sorrow nor your fear.
Go swiftly into blackness
When it finally comes
And weep not for a day which showed no care.
Go swiftly into blackness
When the shadows grow
And night-winds seem to chill your battered frame.
Go swiftly into blackness
When your night appears
And demons of the dark call out your name.
Go swiftly into blackness
When your dues are paid
And grieve not at the thought of what you leave
Go swiftly into blackness
When your daylight fades
For what is gone can never be retrieved.

SIXTY SIX

March 13th

Teach didn't come to see me all day today. I really missed him. I kept looking out the door for him but it wasn't until visiting time was almost over that he finally came hurrying into the room. I tried sulking, pretending to be angry at his lateness but then he showed me a ticket he'd bought me for a Bee Wee flight to Piarco on the 20th. I was so overwhelmed, I held on to his arm and wept.

Suddenly, as if by magic, I could feel the weight of being lost and sick and lonely and homesick fall off my shoulders. Suddenly I realized that for all these years here, I was still a stranger in a strange land; that I never really ceased being a Trini; that I never really made the mental adjustment to life away from home. All I can think of now is returning.

I'm not sure how I'll react when I arrive this time though. It's already eight years since I'd returned for the funerals, and if you remember, I couldn't bring myself to stay, even for a week, afterwards.

I remember how you'd begged me to stay for a while. You'd said that you needed me. But you didn't really need me. You had Hollis. And I couldn't bear the thought of home without Mama and Papa. I still don't know how I'm going to deal with that.

Sometimes, when I recall their devotion to each other, I feel a sense of relief that they were taken together. They never had to suffer the pain and the loneliness of losing your life's companion. With a relationship as long and as close as theirs, it would've been too difficult for the surviving partner to cope.

I know that the house will feel empty without them, but I'll be glad to be home anyway. I hope I won't be a burden to anyone. I know that you'll want me to stay with you and Hollis and the kids but I'll really prefer to stay at home in my old room. And anyway, you'll be only a short distance away if I need you.

Tell the renters that I'll be occupying the upstairs. It's a good thing you only rented-out the downstairs. Have Miss Vilma air it out, and ask her if she'd be willing to work for me while I'm home. Also, make an early appointment for me with Dr Allum. It would be good to have him as my doctor again.

SIXTY SEVEN

Dis morning ah climb dong from mih bed
Mih heart feel so heavy, man ah want to dead
Ah say, Hold strain, ah cyah miss dis fete again
Mih belly start to bun, look ah feelin' bad
When ah study is Joovay in Trinidad.
Ah say, Hold strain, ah cyah miss dis fete again.

Hold strain, look ah done pack ahreddy
Hold strain, ah promise mih baby
Hold strain, dat ah boardin' a Bee Wee
Hold strain, headin' dong to mih country

Right now in Trini d'music nice
While up here ah freezin' in snow and ice.
Ah say, Hold strain, ah cyah miss dis fete again.
D'pressure and d'pain too strong dis time
Ah make up mih mind, ah cyah miss d'lime.
Ah say, Hold strain, ah cyah miss dis fete again.

Hold strain, look ah done pack ahreddy
Hold strain, ah promise mih baby
Hold strain, dat ah boardin' a Bee Wee
Hold strain, headin' dong to mih country

Ah call up d'boss and ah start t'cry
Man ah lie and say how mih Granny die.
Ah say, Hold strain, ah cyah miss dis fete again .
Oh God! Oh God! Travel Agent man,
Get mih dong home any way yuh cyan!
Ah say, Hold strain, ah cyah miss dis fete again.

Hold strain, look ah done pack ahreddy
Hold strain, ah promise mih baby
Hold strain, dat ah boardin' a Bee Wee
Hold strain, headin' dong to mih country

Aye taximan, tell dem clear de way
Doh stop till yuh get mih to JFK
Ah say, Hold strain, ah cyah miss dis fete again
Ah shakin' and ah tremblin' from mih head to toe
Make room on de next flight to Piarco
Ah say Hold strain, ah cyah miss dis fete again.

Hold strain, look ah done pack ahreddy
Hold strain, ah promise mih baby
Hold strain, dat ah boardin' a Bee Wee
Hold strain, headin' dong to mih country

SIXTY EIGHT

March 19th

We left the hospital tonight; Teach and I. We slipped out and nobody even suspected. Ha! Ha! I wish I could see their reaction when they discover that I'm gone.

Dr Timothy and Dr Woo will be very upset when they find out. That is why I didn't indicate my plans to them or to anyone else. Only Teach knew what was going on since he'd planned the whole thing.

During the last few days we made all of our plans in whispers because we didn't want anyone at the hospital to find out. That's why I haven't written. I had to make sure that I didn't betray our scheme in a letter which might fall into the wrong hands here.

As soon as visiting time started today, when a lot of people were moving about, Teach came into the room with his wheel chair. He helped me get on and immediately wheeled me over to the elevator, down to the main lobby and out the front door. He was wearing his uniform so no one gave us a second glance. He placed me in a taxi which he had arranged to be waiting across the street and returned the wheelchair to the hospital lobby. When he rejoined me he had the driver take us to my apartment. No one would miss me for another four hours.

It feels great to be free again! You should've seen us. We were like two children during the entire episode, giggling and whispering between ourselves while still in the hospital, but laughing and talking excitedly in the taxi and at the apartment.

Mrs Kaminsky was shocked when she saw us. She hugged me and wept when I told her that I was going home for a while. She promised to hold my apartment and allow Teach to occupy it until I'm well again and ready to return.

Teach made the taxi driver wait downstairs for us, and while he helped me dress and pack my suitcase, he surprised me by reciting some of my poems from my schooldays; poems that I'd written many years ago. Most of them, I'd forgotten; some I'd misplaced; all he'd shown much appreciation for in the days when he used to critique my work. He had remembered them. I was dumbfounded! He'd remembered all of them!

He's so helpful and considerate to me now! Not only is he going to the airport with me, he'll be waiting there with me to make certain that I'm properly checked in and comfortable in my seat.

SIXTY NINE

His sunken eyes
Like pinpricks pierced my soul,
Flooding my thoughts
With memories of another world.
I hung my head
And trembled in my shame
As a chant rose up
From deep within his broken frame.
It was an old chant;
The final lavway.
I knew his time had come.
I knew he would not stay.

SEVENTY

March 15th

My heart is racing with anticipation. I'm on a new journey. Unknown challenges lie ahead of me again, but now at least I'll face them from the comfort of a known environment.

Except for my time with Joyce, there's not much that I cherish from my life here. The successes of my mainstream years were like shackles on me and my foray into the world of art has been uneventful and unproductive.

Foolishly, I'd abandoned the comfort and security of home and family to pursue a romantic ideal. I'd plunged into murky waters without the faintest idea of how to maneuver. Yet I'd felt that my life was unique; that I was on my way to conquer the world.

I was so convinced of this, that I probably took it all for granted, living my life and pursuing my art with not enough urgency, not enough commitment. I felt that I had something important to say and that one day the whole world would sit up and take notice.

Maybe I was too naïve or I went about it the wrong way or I didn't seize opportunities when they appeared. Or maybe I was just a misplaced Trini who never really belonged away from his roots; who mostly straddled the fence, unwilling to commit fully, reluctant to cut his navel-string.

I'm sure however, that this journey home will offer me an opportunity to re-invent myself; to begin again at the core and forge ahead from the comfort and security of home and family and community.

Throughout my time here and especially after I'd lost Joyce, you were the thread that helped me maintain my sanity and kept me attached to my roots. Your letters have been a constant comfort to me, and for that I'm grateful. I think of you and of home all the time now. I bear only happy memories of our life together, during those early years.

And now, while my body reclines in my window seat here on this BeeWee jet, as it begins its long taxi down the frigid runway, my spirit has already abandoned me and flown on ahead, soaring high above the clouds, winging its way home to you, to Joyce, to Mama and Papa, to my people and to the land I so dearly love.

SEVENTY ONE

"Sorry papa."
"Is okay son."
"I was tired and hungry."
"Me too."
"Papa?"
"Yes?"
"Papa, we was out dere for d'whole day and we eh even ketch one single fish."
"I know."
"But how come?"
"Things doh always work out how we want."
"But it have plenty fish in d'sea. We shoulda ketch at least one."
"D'most we could do is try."
"Papa?"
"Yes son?"
"You think you g'want t'carry mih fishin' with you again?"
"Sure."
"Even doh I geh tired and hungry dis time?"
"Sure son. We stay out dere too long today anyway."

SEVENTY TWO

I asked the river where he goes
Of me he asked the same
I asked the river from where he comes
Of me he asked the same
I asked the river what he'd seen
Of me he asked the same
I asked the river how he felt
Of me he asked the same
I asked the river was he loved
Of me he asked the same
I asked the river why he runs
Of me he asked the same.

EPILOGUE

His body was transferred by the airport authorities to a funeral home in San Fernando.

Afterwards it took four days to get the necessary legal documents before it was released to his sister and her husband Hollis.

A quiet funeral, conducted by the Imam, was held at the family home the next day.

Most of the village people attended including an old couple from up near Kanchan Hill in Caratal. They said that they knew of him through letters from their granddaughter who, at one time, had also lived in America.

His sister fainted during the service and they had to use smelling salts to revive her.

The children wept throughout and even though Hollis tried to console them he too had tears filling his eyes.

No one knew how his childhood friend, Samuel, found out but he showed up too, weeping quietly as he stood off by himself, in the shade of a neighbor's sapodilla tree.

Afterwards he was laid to rest alongside his parents, in the village cemetery on the hill behind the school.

GLOSSARY

All-fours... A card game

Aloo.....Potato.

Bamsee .... Buttocks, bottom, backside, derriere

Baraat .... Wedding procession

Bazodee...... Out of one's head

Bee Wee .... British West Indian Airways

Bhajan...... Hindu religious song

Big people....Adults, grown-ups

Blancoed crepesoles.....Whitened sneakers.

Bobbon cane....Thick sugarcane stalk.

Bobolee ... Fool, idiot

Brakes lash.... Block from being hit

Bulljoll....Dish made from salted dried codfish.

Calaloo....Seasoned porridge made with spinach and ochro.

Carbile.... Carbide chunks used to create a minor explosion

Carat- house ....Thatched-roof house.

Cascadoo .... Cascadura, a fresh water fish native to Trinidad

Cat-cracker ....A catalytic cracking unit at an oil refinery

Chahtow .... A close relative of the cascadura

Chamkay .... Playful, show-off dance

Channa.... Chick peas

Ched-darr .... Bedsheet

Chong-kay ..... Fry

Chook .... Prod

Choolha ... Brick or earthen fireside for cooking

Choonky....Tiny, small

Coob .... Coop, chicken house

Coolie.....Derogatory term for people of Indian descent, once commonly used in Trinidad. Sometimes however, when used among people of similar race or background, as it is here, it can convey a sense of endearment and inclusiveness

Corn coo-coo.... A local dish prepared from cornmeal

Cuchela....Grated un-ripened fruit in mixture of hot spices

Cuss.....Curse, obscene language

Cuss-bud.... One who uses obscene language

Dhal-puree....A flatbread filled with seasoned, ground split-peas

Dharr ..... Holy water

Dhoti.... East Indian loincloth

Dongs .... A small olive-like fruit

Doubles .... Curried chick peas in two flour and saffron patties

Fatigue.... Needling, heckling

Fete ...... Party, celebration

Fo-day morning...... Early dawn

Fraykoon-face .... Very ugly

Hai Ram..... Praise the Lord

Hassah .... Version of the cascadura found in Guyana

Hosay .... Decorated replica of a mosque

Imps .... Fool, idiot

Jamette.... Loose woman

Joovay .... The start of carnival

Jumbie.... Zombie

Kar-hee.... Ground split-pea balls in a curried split-pea sauce

Khalounjee.... Curried stuffed bitter melons (karela or karaili)

Kitchree.... Seasoned lentils and rice cook-down combination

Krestles..... Watercress

Kurta..... East Indian men's shirt

Kutya .... Shrine

Like Mama dog in heat… Very aggressive
Lime….. Hang out, a light-hearted gathering
Lotah….. Brass goblet
Mahrr….Left-over water from boiled rice
Mala…..Garland
Mamaguy …. Fool, flatter
Mamataytah…. Suckermouth catfish
Mandir….Hindu temple
Manicou …. Opossum
Manjay … Scrub, clean
Marazmee…. A debilitating sickness
Mas … Masquerade
Merrymaid…..Mermaid
Mop…. Beg for
Never-see-come-see….One who's unaccustomed to some things
Nigger…..Derogatory term for people of African descent, once commonly used in Trinidad. Sometimes however, when used among people of similar race or background, as it is here, it can convey a sense of endearment and inclusiveness.
Oak…. Abbreviation for Old Oak, a brand of rum
Old mas …. A big commotion
Pahgree….Turban
Pahyol … Spanish
Pandit…. Hindu priest
Pappy-show …. Camouflage, show-off, spectacle
Paymee….Sweet pastelle made from cornmeal
Peenee…..Skinny, small
Pelau….Dish made with rice, pigeon peas, meat and seasonings
Pelt lash…. Swing with intention to hit or strike
Pico ….Picoplat, a small songbird
Picong …. Needling, heckling
Pommerack…..Tropical pear-shaped fruit

Poo-yah .... Cutlass, machete
Poolowrie.... Small, fried turmeric-flavored dough balls
Pudden .... Fried pudding made from seasoned animal blood
Puncheon .... Extra-strong white (clear) rum
Puss-pussing..... Gossiping, whispering
Put down.... Give birth
Rag-up.... Make fun of, laugh at, heckle
Ram-cram.... Full, overflowing
Roti.... East Indian flatbread
Ruckshun..... Noise and commotion
Sago pap ..... Tapioca pudding
Saheena.... Fried patty made from ground split peas and spinach
Shak-shak.... Maracas, rattles made from gourds.
Sulwah .... Gravy, sauce
Tal-karee.... *Cooked vegetables*
Tambran.... Tamarind
Tantee ...... Auntie
Tariah .... Brass plate
Taska road.... Cane-field gravel road
Tassa.... East Indian goatskin drum
Tiger-wire..... Barb wire
Tooloom.... Candy made with molasses and coconut
Tum-tum.... Seasoned mashed bananas
Vat.... Vat 19, a brand of rum
Wahbeen.... A local fresh water fish, similar to a trout
Warahoons .... Aborigine Indians
Whales .... Welts
What monkey see monkey do.... Mimic, copy
Whole road.... The entire distance